ALPHA'S HUNGER

A DARK PARANORMAL ROMANCE

RENEE ROSE

RENEE ROSE ROMANCE

WANT FREE RENEE ROSE BOOKS?

tion, Theirs to Protect, Owned by the Marine and more. In addition to the free stories, you will also get bonus epilogues, special pricing, exclusive previews and news of new releases.

FOREWORD

Dearest reader,

When the publishing rights to the *Alpha Doms* series returned to me from Stormy Night Publications, the original publisher, I considered a major re-edit / re-write, as I'd done with my *Made Men* series. It's been nearly ten years since *The Alpha's Hunger* was published, and my writing ability, style, and content have evolved significantly. I still love kink, but I've moved away from the punishy-style, keeping it more in the sexy realm.

In the end, I decided to leave the series as is—a picture in time. Humbling though it may be to me, by leaving it as is, you can see my evolution as a storyteller. *The Alpha's Hunger* (2015) is my billionaire boss wolf shifter 1.0., *Alpha's Temptation* (2017) became 2.0 and *Big Bad Boss* (2024) is 3.0. Who knows what shape 4.0 will take?

As always, I am eternally grateful to you, the reader, who keeps me writing, pushing my craft, and learning to find new depth with each story I tell. Thank you for your readership now, and if you've been with me since the beginning, a million kisses for sticking with me all this time.

1

Ben hit the button for the parking garage on the elevator and rubbed his face. As the unit plunged down the shaft, the hairs on the back of his neck stood on end. His instincts warned him to pay attention.

To what? He looked up to read which floor he was passing and without thinking, hit the next one. The elevator stopped and the doors slid open. He put his foot against one side to hold it open, listening. His skin prickled. Yes, someone or something was here.

He stepped out, keeping his movements silent. Most of the lights were off, computer screens on screensaver. By seven-thirty, all five hundred twenty-three of his employees had left for the night. He rounded a corner and his senses sharpened when he caught sight of a woman's arm lying on the floor, extending from one of the cubicles. He surged forward, the adrenaline already causing him to partially shift.

A young woman lay sprawled on her back on the floor, eyes closed. What in the—? As he lunged to kneel at her side, her eyes fluttered open and she shrieked. She scrambled up to stand. "M-Mr. Stone!"

He grasped her arms and lifted her to her feet, taking a deep breath and willing his vision back to normal. Something about the feel of her flesh under his palms made it harder to relax. He released her. Still, the hairs stood up on his arms, his instincts screaming for his attention. Why? What danger lay here?

"What happened?"

"Oh, nothing!" the young woman exclaimed, smoothing her long reddish-brown waves back from her face. "I just… I have a migraine, and it affects my vision, so I didn't want to drive. I was trying to meditate it away." She spoke quickly, no doubt flustered to have the company's owner and CEO in her cubicle. "I'm sorry, I'm sure it looked like I'd fainted or collapsed. I didn't mean to alarm you." Her blue eyes appeared shrunken with pain, but even so, her beauty was undeniable. High cheekbones, big eyes, and a wide, sensual mouth. As he looked at her lips, his vision domed again, bringing the peripheral into focus along with her face. He blinked, pushing back the threatened change, hoping his irises hadn't changed color. She didn't appear to have noticed anything. Strange... no human woman—hell, no female at all had ever had such an effect on him.

Too gruffly, he demanded, "Do you work here?"

The acrid scent of fear told him he'd made her nervous. Which was nothing new. The employees of Stone Technologies had learned in the three years of his reign to watch their step around him. He had little tolerance for any of them. He knew what they called him: Stone Man. Because he never smiled.

"Yes, Mr. Stone. This is my office. I'm a marketing assistant." She grabbed a framed photo of herself and a girl who looked identical to her and held it up. "See? This is my desk."

"You can't have security clearance. How did you plan to lock up when you left after hours?"

Her eyes widened. "Well, Steve is still working down in R&D. He said I could stay as long as he was here."

For some reason the thought of her getting cozy with anyone named Steve—whoever he may be—made him want to tear the man's throat out. He gave himself a shake. What was wrong with him?

"What's your name?"

"Ashley. Ashley Bell." She held out her hand.

"Ben Stone." He took her palm, once more experiencing a strange reaction to touching her skin. Heat tingled in at the contact, shooting up his arm.

"I know," she said with a smile.

He yanked his hand back, unsettled by his reaction to the slip of a human female. "Get your things. I'll drive you home," he said curtly.

Her expressive mouth rounded into a little *O*. "Um, that's not necessary, Mr. Stone. I can call a friend, or a cab, or—" She broke off at his stern gaze. "All right," she said meekly. He caught a whiff of another smell, mixed in with the fear: arousal.

He stiffened. For him? The wolf in him surged and he had to steady his breath.

Ashley opened a drawer and grabbed her purse. A paperback book fell to the floor.

He retrieved it before she could snatch it up.

"Oh, that's—"

He turned it over to look at the cover. A man with a naked torso and washboard abs graced the front, wind blowing his shoulder-length hair. A romance reader. Cute.

"That's… not mine," she said lamely, a pretty blush coloring her cheeks.

His mouth twitched in a smile. "Right," he said, handing it back with a raised eyebrow that caused her to blush again.

She shoved it in her purse and licked her lips. The sight of her tongue sent a pulse of heat to his cock. He took another breath and blew it out slowly, trying to understand what was happening. The girl was human, he was sure of it. Not his destined mate. Weak. Fragile. Not even able to withstand a marking. How could she be calling up his most base desires when no female—human or wolf alike—had ever done so?

He touched her back to let her pass and he thought he felt her shiver, the scent of arousal growing stronger. She stole a glance at him from under her lashes.

Closed in the elevator with her, her scent filled his nostrils. She wore a rich, vanilla fragrance, but it was her own natural scent underneath that made his blood warm. He wanted to touch her again, wanted to soften the line between her brows, the one that betrayed her pain.

Get a grip, Ben.

"So, how long have you worked for me?"

She looked up, her lips forming a pretty bow. "Almost two years."

"Do you like it?"

She hesitated a beat. "Yes, yes, of course."

"What don't you like?"

"I said I like it," she protested.

"You're not the best liar."

She flushed. "I'm really happy here. I'm just," she licked her lips again, "looking forward to taking on more responsibility."

He rewarded her with a glimmer of a smile.

"Very diplomatic, Ashley. I appreciate that. It's a skill I lack."

She smiled and looked down at her feet as if to hide it. Clearly she'd heard all the rumors about him.

"So you're bored?"

The elevator doors opened, giving him the opportunity to touch her back again to escort her out. Her hips swayed, heels clicking on the concrete.

"No… well, honestly? Yes. But I understand I have to work my way up. And I'm willing to do it."

"I might have a personal assistant position opening up on the top floor, if you're interested." He didn't know what made him say it. His secretary had been trying to act as a personal assistant to him since the day he'd taken over the company after his brother's death, and he'd been pushing her away. But something about Ashley Bell intoxicated him. He couldn't have her, but he wanted to keep her near, even if it meant giving up his coveted privacy and solitude.

Her eyes slid sideways. "Is that a glorified secretarial position?"

He resisted the urge to swat her sashaying backside. "Do you think it's beneath you? I assure you the pay is at least twice, maybe three times what you're making now."

"No, I—" She blushed again.

He wanted to push her against his black Mustang and kiss her full lips.

"I'm sorry, that was rude. Would I be working for you?"

"Yes… do you find that daunting?"

She let out a short bark of laughter. "Yes," she admitted. "But it would also be the main selling point."

Her answer pleased him more than he wanted to admit. He needed to regain his footing. "Am I selling this job to you?" he asked drily.

"Oh—" Her smile vanished. "Of course not. I-I would be honored to be considered for the position, of course."

He caught another whiff of her arousal. Was she turned on by his sternness? The same thing that made his employees complain about him? Wolves responded to dominance, but humans were a mixed bag. While he could make every one of his employees grovel with little more than a disapproving look, not all of them enjoyed submitting. This one, it seemed, lived for it. Maybe that was his attraction to her.

He opened the passenger side door for her and watched her shapely legs as she folded them into the car. When he climbed in beside her, he asked for her address and put it in his GPS. Then he began to grill her. "Education?"

"Bachelor's in English/film studies from Colorado College."

"Grade point average?"

"Three point eight seven, magna cum laude, Phi Beta Kappa."

"Work history?"

"Three years as a barista at Starbucks, two years as waitress at Red Lobster. One internship with Channel Four News. Close to two years here."

"How old are you?"

"Twenty-five." She rubbed her temples.

He instantly regretted giving her the third degree. "I'm sorry, he said, softening his tone. "Am I making your head worse?" He realized she'd grown paler since they'd left the building.

"No," she said, but he knew it was a lie.

"We don't have to talk," he said.

He muted the guidance system and followed the map, driving in silence until he reached her brick duplex in the hip but transitional Denver neighborhood.

"I'll pick you up in the morning. Be ready by seven."

Her mouth dropped. "What? Really?"

He wrote his cell phone number on the back of a card. "Call me if the migraine will keep you from going to work."

She blinked at him, looking stunned. "You're picking me up? In the morning?"

"Well, you left your car in the parking garage, didn't you?"

"Yes, but—"

He waved his hand impatiently with his usual rudeness, shooing her out of his car.

"Thank you, Mr. Stone."

"Good night," he said curtly, putting the car into gear before she even shut the door.

He needed to leave before he followed her in and tore her clothes off, marked her with his teeth, and claimed the little human… He shook his head. That couldn't happen. Because she wouldn't forgive it, for one thing. And he didn't do relationships, for another. No, this very strange development, this sudden interest in a female human could not be pursued. Period.

He sighed and rubbed his palm over his face, her scent still lingering in his nostrils.

DESPITE THE THROBBING in her head, Ashley's senses zinged from contact with Ben Stone. Talk about magnetism. Some said he had the personality of an ice cube, but all she'd sensed was pure masculine power. Even through his crisp designer suit, she'd seen the outline of sculpted muscles in his arms and chest. His dark, Latino looks dripped sexual prowess and the silence made him mysterious. And those pale green eyes had seemed to flicker to amber under the fluorescent lights at the office…

She dropped her things and started a bath, filling a washcloth with ice for the back of her neck. Heat on the body, cold on the head. Not that it ever worked. Nothing helped when she had a migraine. Her phone rang and she looked to see who was calling. Melissa—her twin sister. She hit talk. "Hey, how's it going?"

Melissa lived two hours away in Colorado Springs, but they still spoke almost every day.

"Do you have a headache?"

"How can you tell?"

"Your voice gets all tight. I'm sorry. Did you try the hot bath, cold washcloth thing?"

"Trying it now. I'm taking you into the bathtub with me."

"Just don't drop your phone, you might get electrocuted or something," Melissa teased.

She snorted. "I think that's just with hairdryers." She pulled her clothes off and stepped in the tub. "You'll never believe who just took me home."

"Who?"

"Ben Stone, the CEO and owner of Stone Tech."

Melissa whistled. "Nice. How'd you swing that?"

She told her sister the whole story, from him

finding her lying on the floor in her cubicle to telling her he had a personal assistant position open.

"So, what's he like?"

"Super sexy in that dark, brooding Batman sort of way."

"Did he say *I'm Stoneman?*" her sister asked, attempting a deep, throaty voice.

She giggled. "I wish I hadn't had this migraine, because I screwed up my chances at the position by putting my foot in my mouth."

"I don't know, Ash. He's picking you up in the morning. It kinda sounds to me like you have this one nailed."

She tried to ignore the frissons of excitement her sister's words caused. "I definitely wouldn't say that. He's a tough nut to crack. Totally unreadable."

"What's the scoop on him, anyway? He's South American, right? And he moved here to run the company when his brother died?"

"Yeah, I read in *Business Weekly* that he's half Latino. His mom was American and that's where the name Stone comes from. He graduated from Harvard Business School and he's only thirty. That's about all I know. The company has sort of languished since Ben's been CEO, but he refuses to step down and hire someone more experienced to run it even though the board has been pushing for it. He still owns the majority interest, so they can't fire him."

"So, you think he'll get things figured out?"

"Well, he's smart enough. Some people say he doesn't care about the company, but I'm not sure that's true. I don't know, but I sure would like the chance to get close enough to him to form an opinion."

"Well, tell him tomorrow when he picks you up."

"Tell him what?"

"That you really want the job."

Her pulse quickened just at the thought of sitting beside him in his car again. "Okay," she said.

"You're not going to," her sister accused, probably catching the nervous twinge in her voice.

"No, I will. I will. You're right. It's worth groveling over."

"So, guess who's coming over here tonight?"

"Ooh, who?"

"Donny. The guy I met at the roller derby meet. Remember I was telling you about him?"

"Of course I remember." She couldn't always keep track—her sister was a bit of a serial dater. "That's awesome. What are you going to do?"

"We're just going to watch a movie we talked about that night we met."

"Mmm hmm. Sure you're just going to watch a movie," she teased.

"Well, if stuff happens in the dark, I'm not going to call 9-1-1 or anything," Melissa said with a laugh.

They chatted a little more and she hung up, leaning her head back against the cool porcelain of the tub, the ice tucked up behind her neck. This migraine had better be gone by tomorrow morning because there was no way she was missing out on another ride with Ben Stone.

THE NEXT MORNING, she changed five times before she finally settled on a short, fitted skirt and silk blouse. Her headache had mostly disappeared, although the aura of it still made her face feel tight and her eyes appear too small. She stood at the window of her duplex, ready to go by 6:45 a.m.

Even so, when the black Mustang pulled up, she snatched up her things and dashed out as if she were late. Ben was just getting out of his car when she came flying down the porch steps to the side-walk. He stopped, leaning against the car, gazing at her with a speculative look. "Good morning, Ashley."

"Good morning, Mr. Stone," she said breathlessly.

She opened the car door and got in, holding her satchel primly in front of her. She suddenly wished she owned a nicer briefcase, not this old leather schoolbag that made her look young and immature.

"How's your head?"

"Better," she said, forcing a bright smile.

He scanned her face. "Not quite," he said.

Her smile dimmed. "Mostly," she said, oddly defensive.

The corner of his mouth twitched.

Her heart picked up speed. Did the man who never smiled find her amusing? She hoped, rather desperately, that he did.

"So… I, uh, wanted to apologize for that secretary comment I made yesterday. I didn't mean to sound like a spoiled brat."

Again, the twitch of his mouth as his eyes slid sideways to meet hers.

She caught her breath when their gazes locked and held, his dark-lashed green eyes melting her with each suspended moment. He looked back to the road and the spell broke.

She exhaled and tried again. "I hope you'll still consider me for the position. I mean, I'd like to interview for it, or submit my application or whatever the process is…" She trailed off. She wasn't usually this tongue-tied, but she found the gruff CEO more than a little intimidating. Which was half of the appeal. The other half being his brooding good looks and the power of his position.

"Three o'clock, my office."

"Really? For an interview?"

He didn't answer that question, as if he only had a certain allotment of words each day and he didn't want to hit his limit answering stupid questions from her. She sat back in the seat and watched the skillful way he navigated traffic.

"Thank you for picking me up today." *Lame, Ashley. Very lame.*

He didn't even look at her this time.

Right. *Keep your mouth shut, Ash.*

When they reached the building, he pulled into his reserved spot, right by the elevators.

"Thanks again," she said as they stepped into the elevator together.

He didn't answer, but his eyes were on her face again, studying her. Her cheeks grew warm. His mouth twitched. "Where are you from?"

"Oh," she said, drawing a breath to recover from the scrutiny of his gaze. "Here. Lakewood," she said, naming the suburb of Denver where she'd grown up.

He nodded.

"Sports? Activities?"

"I took State in swimming in high school," she offered hopefully.

This won an almost smile.

The elevator arrived on her floor. "Well, um, thanks again. I'll see you at three. I mean, I'm looking forward to our meeting," she said, backing out of the elevator.

Only his eyebrow moved in acknowledgment. The doors slid shut and she exhaled, smiling as she walked to her cubicle. She had landed the interview. Now she just had to figure out how to impress him. What did Mr. Stone like in an employee? She feared there was no one at Stone Technologies who knew the answer to that question.

BEN DIDN'T HAVE a clue what he would do with a personal assistant. He didn't like anyone in his business or his space. He didn't want to hear their whispers or smell their smells. He didn't want to have to talk to them. What had possessed him to invent a personal assistant job? Ashley Bell, obviously. For whatever reason, he wanted to keep her close at hand.

Her scent still lingered, filling his mind with images of stripping her naked. He wanted to sink his teeth into her shoulder while he plowed into her from behind, hard and fast. But she was human. Hell, even if she was a shifter, with Carlos Sandoval out to kill him, he was not mate material.

He sighed and picked up his phone, asking Karen, his secretary, to make the arrangements to add a workstation to the office next to his.

"Yes, sir," she replied, knowing better than to ask him who or what it was for.

He leaned back in his chair, put his feet up on the desk, and opened Ashley's personnel file. It contained very little—her resume, application, references. Well, what had he expected, a life history?

He opened his computer and searched for her name on the Internet. It produced three references —one from her high school swimming championship and two from her college academic achievements. He searched her name on Facebook and perused her photos, which she unwisely shared with the public. The same girl from the photo she'd flashed him in his office appeared in many of them —a sister almost identical to her, except for the cut of her hair. They must be twins. Her relationship status was listed as single and very few guys appeared in the photos, which was fortunate, because he might have hunted down any man pretending to be good enough for her.

Karen called to say his top level management team had arrived for the morning meeting, so he picked up his coffee mug and headed to the conference room.

Jack, his brother's best friend and vice president of development met him at the door with the same disapproving, pinched expression he always wore. Jack hated that Ben had taken the helm of the company and, in his opinion, was running it into the ground. The programmer had been part of the company since its initial start-up. Jack had helped design the first game software and been at Leon's side during the lean years, helping him to grow it and get it where it was now.

When Leon died, Ben had thought about turning his share of the stock over to Jack and letting him have the company, just as he'd refused to take leadership of his brother's pack, but in the end, it didn't seem right. His brother had left the company stock to him rather than to his wife and young children, which told him something. If Leon had trusted Jack to run the company, he would've left the stock to Shayla, presuming she and their children would be cared for. By leaving it to Ben, it meant Leon needed Ben there to look after things, to ensure the profits continued for the benefit of his family. And so Ben was there, running a multi-million dollar company with no experience. But he owed his brother. If he had done his duty in the first place, Leon would still be alive.

He went into the meeting and listened as the team presented their weekly reports, which were dismal, as usual. Suma Games was rapidly taking over Stone's market share. When he questioned the causes, he got excuses. In the first year, he had believed them, still getting his bearings and the culture of the company. Now he'd come to recognize the bullshit, but he hadn't figured out what to do about it yet. As he stacked the reports in front of him, he hatched an idea.

When Karen buzzed him that afternoon to say Ashley had arrived, he told her to send her to the conference room. He picked up the reports his management team supplied him with and entered.

She jumped to her feet, knocking her rolling chair backward.

"Sit."

"Woof," she said.

He arched a brow, hiding his amusement. No one talked back to him at Stone Technologies, but for some reason, on her, he found it cute.

She blushed. "Sorry," she mumbled, settling back into her chair. "I was just making a joke…"

He walked around to the seat opposite her, but sat on the table rather than a chair, dropping the sales reports and financial data in front of her. "Sales are down. Costs are up. Find me ten strategies to rectify the situation and you have the job."

She gaped at him, her blue eyes wide. "Um… okay." She picked up the papers and began leafing through them. Her tongue darted out to lick her lips and he nearly groaned at the sight.

"You have one hour. Two if you need it."

She exhaled. "Okay. Got it. Thank you."

"Thank you, *sir*."

Her jaw dropped momentarily before she

snapped it shut and blushed again. "Thank you, sir. I'm sorry, I don't know the right etiquette, or protocol or whatever, but I'll learn. I'm a quick learner."

"I'm sure you are," he said, standing up from his perch on the table and walking out.

He left her alone for an hour, then another. At five o'clock he opened the door to the conference room and found Ashley sweating, the reports and papers spread out in front of her.

She jumped up.

"Sit."

"Woof."

This time he actually smiled. He couldn't help it. That she had tried her joke a second time after failing the first showed a confidence and resiliency he admired.

When she caught his smile, her face broke into a wide grin.

Torn between wanting to stare at its brilliance and needing to shut her down before she gained any further footing, he looked down at the papers. "Well?"

"I only found eight," she said immediately, clicking the top of her pen. "But I'm sure I can find two more if you give me just a little more time."

He hadn't really expected her to find ten. Hell, he hadn't expected her to find more than three. "Tell me what you've got."

Ashley picked up a piece of notebook paper where she'd made a list. "The first one is phasing out the NE3 Game Stations. A lot of money goes into maintaining them, when if you'd just refuse to service them any longer, everyone would buy the E6's."

He nodded. The idea had occurred to him as well, but he hadn't acted on it, mainly because the NE3 had been his brother's first product, the platform for Robo Shooters, and the company, himself included, clung to it with a sentimental attachment. Hearing confirmation of his instinct from Ashley made up his mind. "Next."

"Um…" She looked down at her paper. "Costs on a number of these products seem too high, considering what we're charging. The profit margin isn't large enough. I suggest we institute a cost reduction team, awarding prizes to engineers or teams who can reduce by the most."

He liked the way she used the word 'we,' if they were already a team. It was presumptuous, yet it sounded right coming from her lips. "Good," he said, throwing her a bone.

She lifted her eyes at the compliment, then looked at her paper once more. "My third suggestion is to recover the market we lost to Suma Games last year. This is sort of a two-part suggestion, so I counted it as number three and number four." She raised her gaze again, as if checking to see if he would allow it.

He nodded.

"So, the first would be an advertising campaign. And the second would be product development to compete with their D-boy unit. I understand both of those will require an outlay of capital, but I do think the investment would be worth it."

He didn't comment.

"Okay," she said, drawing another breath. "Number five is to thin out some of middle management." She stopped, watching his face for a reaction.

"Reasoning?"

"Right. Um, the reasoning is that you have an awful lot of people who sit around here and don't do anything but tell others what to do and report further up the chain."

"Speaking from experience?"

She hesitated. "Yes, sir."

He liked that she remembered to call him *sir*.

"Number six?"

She continued, describing her last three ideas, of which all but one seemed sound.

When she finished, he let her sit for a moment while he contemplated her in silence.

"So, as I said, I'm sure I can come up with two more—"

"Yes. I will expect you to. You can think about it

tonight. You'll start tomorrow. Karen will show you your new office."

Her face split into a grin. "Mr. Stone! Thank you. You won't be disappointed, I promise."

He tapped the table. "See that I'm not." He started for the door and stopped when he reached it. "Type up those suggestions and send them to me in an email, along with the backup data."

"Yes, sir," she said, still beaming.

He walked out, shaking his head, not at her, but at himself. Inviting her into his personal space was courting disaster.

2

Ashley arrived at work the next morning by 7:15, since she knew Ben arrived at 7:30. Karen, his secretary, was already there, her French twist in perfect order, her manicured nails tapping on the keyboard.

"Good morning," Ashley said breathlessly. "I baked some banana bread." She set it on the counter of the wet bar.

"I don't eat wheat," Karen said without looking up.

"Oh," she said, deflating slightly. "I'll make it with rice flour next time. It tastes just as good—even better, really."

"That's all right. I don't eat in the morning."

So eat it for lunch.

She squared her shoulders and headed for her

office. The top floor was set up with Ben's large windowed office in the corner, and smaller offices all around, all empty, except for hers. Karen sat at the reception desk outside. From what she understood, when Leon Stone had worked here, these offices all contained top managers—the CFO and vice presidents—but Ben had moved them all down a level when he took over because he liked the quiet. Obviously it hadn't been a popular move, and had set the tone for his leadership.

She had packed the things from her office on the fifth floor into a box the night before, so she began unpacking now, pinning pictures and cards to her bulletin board, and setting up framed photos.

The elevator dinged and Mr. Stone emerged. She lifted her chin and hurried out. "Good morning, Mr. Stone. I baked some banana bread if you'd like some. It has chocolate chips."

His green eyes raked over her with a curious glint, but his "No," was about as curt as it gets.

"No, thank you?" she corrected. She didn't know what made her dare it—just disappointment and frustration at the rebuff, she supposed.

He stopped in his tracks, a muscle tightening in his jaw. "Is it your place to teach me manners, Ms. Bell?"

She felt the blood drain from her face as her body went cold. "No, sir."

Then she saw it—the faint lift in one corner of his mouth. "No, thank you," he amended and continued into his office. A shiver of excitement ran through her. What was that? Were they flirting? Why did she find his gruffness so darn appealing?

She exhaled.

Karen was looking at her with laughter in her expression.

Not sure whether she was laughing at her or with her, she braved a return smile, trying for rueful. "I'll be lucky if I make it through the day, at this rate," she said.

Karen seemed as silent as her boss, only smirking.

"I can't believe I got the job. How many people applied?"

"I think he must have created it for you," the older woman said, looking at her speculatively. "If you want to last, don't stay out here and chit-chat. He hates noise. That was why he moved all the other offices downstairs."

"Okaaay," she said. "Got it. Thanks."

She walked to her office. How would she survive up here with no one to talk to? She was, for the most part, a very social creature.

She finished organizing her desk, which didn't take long, since her cubicle downstairs had been tiny. This big office, with the windows overlooking downtown Denver, seemed stark and empty. She would need to buy some paintings for the walls or something.

Her phone rang and she jumped, knocking the receiver over before she picked it up. "This is Ashley."

"Come into my office."

"Oh, ah, yes, sir," she said. She started to put it down, then returned it to her ear to listen. Does one say 'goodbye' in this situation? The line was dead. Okay, clearly not. She grabbed a notebook and pen and headed into his office.

"Sit," he said.

She didn't attempt her doggy joke again as she settled into the chair across his desk.

"Thank you for the report, and the additional ideas you sent at," he checked his computer screen, "five in the morning."

Did she sense faint amusement there? She flushed. "I'm excited about this job."

He touched his fingers together. "I'm glad." His face looked anything but glad, the firm lines of his jaw looking as stony as usual. "I'd like to begin to implement some of your suggestions. Arrange a meeting with the advertising agency to talk about our new campaign and get me a list of your recommended cuts from middle management."

She gaped. "Um... okay. So, do I invite sales and marketing to the advertising meeting?"

He cocked his head. "What do you think?"

She licked her lips and found his eyes on her mouth. Her heart picked up speed. Did he find her attractive? The idea came as one part thrilling and one part disappointing. If she'd landed this job only because he wanted to get into her pants… She shifted in her chair. Not that she was entirely opposed to letting him in her pants. Or skirt, as the case may be.

With effort, she dragged her mind back to the rather overwhelming issues at hand. "Well…"

"Talk through it out loud," he said, circling his finger in the air. "I want to hear how you think."

Okay, maybe she had won this position fair and square.

"Well, I'm thinking they bring a certain close-mindedness to things. I mean, they're set in their ways about what they think we should be doing, and we're trying to do something new. On the other hand, to go around them would totally ruffle feathers and make it harder to get buy-in."

Mr. Stone regarded her with cool assessment. Not surprisingly, he said nothing.

"I guess, selfishly, I'd rather keep them out, at least initially, because I'm afraid all my ideas will get trashed."

"I appreciate your honesty, Ms. Bell."

She rubbed her lips together. "So what do you think?"

"The choice is yours."

She gaped. "The choice is mine?"

He nodded. "Make a good one."

Oh, God.

She looked down at her notebook where she'd written down his direction. "And for the second one —I'm not sure I'm qualified to make that sort of assessment."

"Well, do what you need to do to get qualified. I'm asking you to make it."

"That's a pretty huge responsibility; I mean, you want me to make a recommendation that affects people's livelihoods."

"And the future of this company. Welcome to my world, Ms. Bell. Do you want to be my assistant or not?"

She flushed and looked down at her paper to compose herself. "I do," she said quietly. "I appreciate your faith in me." When he said nothing, she amended, "Or maybe this is a test, in which case, I plan to pass it." She lifted her chin.

A smile flashed around both corners of his mouth, but it disappeared as quickly as it had come. "Go," he said, with his characteristic curtness.

She stood and walked to the door. Grasping the knob, she screwed up her courage and turned around. "Mr. Stone?"

He turned from his computer screen and raised an eyebrow.

"Did you hire me for this job because you actually think I show promise or is it because—" She stopped.

He didn't help, gazing at her with both eyebrows raised now.

She swallowed. "Because you like the way I look in a skirt?"

The smile flitted across his face and his eyes dropped to her skirt and down her legs.

She flushed, wishing she hadn't said it.

"Get out, Ashley."

She actually laughed. Well, it was more a gasp for breath, or a sob. But it came out like a bubble of laughter. He'd called her by her first name, which felt like a success. And she loved the way it sounded in his deep, rich tones, evoking intimacy and… heat. She pushed the door open and stumbled out, relieved to be out of his intense presence. But the moment she shut the door, she missed it.

How would she survive working for this man? He stole her breath with every glance.

JACK CAME into his office without an invite and plopped into the chair opposite him. "What's with the new girl?"

For some reason it bothered him Jack called her

a girl. "Ashley Bell. She's my new assistant. She was working in marketing."

"Hmm." Jack looked at him.

He knew what he was thinking. It was what Karen thought. Even Ashley thought it. He found a hot piece of tail and he wanted her to parade in and out of his office in short skirts to brighten his day.

Well, hell. It might be true. Every time he caught her scent, his body heated like it wanted to mark her. But she wasn't just a pretty face. The girl had all kinds of bright ideas, and her fearlessness intrigued him. He didn't know why he, a natural alpha, had been such a nancy at running this company. Not at managing the people, but at making changes and shaking things up. Ashley's ideas all affirmed his natural instincts, which he had been ignoring.

He shrugged. "She's brilliant. I don't know why her talent wasn't being put to better use, but it is now."

"I see," Jack said drily.

The hairs on the back of his neck bristled, but he drew a deep breath to regain his temper. "What do you need, Jack?"

"Listen, I've been thinking. Everyone knows you don't really love running this company. I'm willing to buy out your share of the company. I mean, I don't have the money now, but I think we could come to an arrangement—some kind of payment plan for the controlling interest. You and Leon's family would be taken care of for life, and I would take over the nitty-gritty of running things."

Jack had suggested this before. Ben didn't know why he was trying it again.

"No."

Jack's face flushed, his eyes narrowing. "You don't know anything about running a gaming company. You're taking us into the ground. Suma Games is about to run us over and everyone on the board of directors knows it."

He swallowed back a growl, standing up. The alpha in him wanted to threaten Jack's job, but the truth was, losing Jack would be a huge blow to the company. He steadied his breath. "I'm about to start making changes," he said, putting a note of warning in his voice. "I have no intention of leaving this company or running it into the ground, so get used to my leadership."

Jack stood up, the muscle under his right eye twitching. "You have no clue what you're doing," he said as he stalked to the door.

Ben didn't answer, but he gave him the alpha stare all the way out the door.

When Jack had disappeared in the elevator, Ben left his office and walked into Ashley's.

"Hi," she said, flashing him that brilliant smile.

She had perfect teeth, gleaming white between her glossed lips.

He liked that she didn't jump to her feet or look ruffled this time. As if they already had a casual relationship, where one of them leaned against the doorway of the other's office. He did just that, folding his arms over his chest. "What did you decide about the advertising meeting?"

"I invited them," she said, looking slightly defeated. "My own ego is far less important than getting cohesiveness back in this company, especially where you're concerned."

His eyebrows shot up to his forehead. "What do you mean *back* in this company?"

She flushed. "I just mean, from what I've heard, the company has lost morale and divided into factions in the past few years."

"Since I took over, you mean."

"Yes." She met his eye.

He admired her courage in telling him the truth. "So you think it's important for me to stroke some egos?"

"Well," she said thoughtfully, rising from her chair and coming to sit on the opposite side of her desk, facing him.

Her scent enervated him, and the sight of her long legs crossed loosely at the ankles fired a jolt of lust through him.

"I think there's a delicate balance. It isn't your

role to stroke egos, necessarily, but if people don't feel like you're looking for their valuable contribution, they'll just get in the way. You want them working hard to please you."

I definitely want you working hard to please me. "I certainly do," he said.

She must've caught his thoughts because her eyes shot to his, widening slightly. Her pupils dilated when their gazes locked and he caught that heady whiff of her arousal.

She tore her gaze away, touching her lips with her fingertips, and looking over her shoulder at her desk, as if something important might be there. "Anyway, I figure if my ideas get stomped on, I can always campaign privately with you."

He wondered what a private campaign would look like. Strip tease in his office with the door shut? The image of her crawling across his desk on her hands and knees rose in his mind, unbidden. Damn. He needed to get a grip.

She's not a shifter.

"That's awfully cocky of you," he murmured.

She flushed, but must be catching onto his humor, because she smiled. "I'm sure you'll be putting me in my place on an hourly basis."

For the first time in ages, he laughed—actually threw his head back and laughed. "Count on it," he said, still smiling as he walked out.

Karen watched him emerge with interest. He

supposed the sound of his laughter would be completely foreign to her.

Ashley slipped out of her dripping swimsuit and dried off in the YMCA locker room. Before she became Ben's assistant she swam in the mornings before work. Now she got to work so early that she had to go in the evenings, sometimes quite late.

Not that she minded. Her first week had already given her the most exciting work of her life. Only working for the president of the United States could be more interesting and thrilling than working for Ben Stone. Hell, he exuded as much power as she imagined the head of state did, maybe more.

Her cell phone buzzed and she dived for it. She'd been trying to get ahold of Melissa for the entire day and it was odd for her sister not to at least text her back. She smiled when she saw the screen. It was Melissa.

"Hey, where have you been?"

An electronically disguised male voice spoke into her ear. "We have your sister."

She caught the phone as it fell from her fingers. "W-what?"

"You will find a laptop on your kitchen table. Replace Ben Stone's with that one. Meet us in the northwest corner of the third floor of the parking garage at 7 p.m. tomorrow night and bring Stone's computer. If you tell anyone, your sister's dead."

"Ashley, I'm all—!" her sister's voice, calling out from a distance to the phone, cut off.

"What have you done to my sister?" she snarled, rage taking over her initial shock.

"Shut up. If you want to see your sister alive you will do everything we tell you to do."

The phone line went dead. She jabbed the buttons, calling back, but of course it went straight to voicemail, as it had all day. Damn.

She threw her clothes on, her entire body trembling. What in the hell was going on? What did they want with Ben's laptop? And where did they have her sister? Did they mean they would trade her sister for the laptop?

She yanked her phone back out of her bag and texted: *I will not give the laptop until you release my sister.*

She stared at the screen after hitting send, but of course, no answer appeared. Without bothering to blow-dry her hair, she picked up her gym bag and jogged out to her car. They said the laptop was on her kitchen table. That meant they'd been in her house.

Should she call the police?

If you tell anyone, your sister's dead.

She wanted to call Ben Stone. It seemed like he would know what to do, and besides, this seemed to involve him. But they were probably monitoring her phone calls.

Melissa. The thought of her sister being hurt or scared made her chest tighten painfully. No wonder she'd been worried all day. Her twin intuition had been going off.

She drove home, speeding the entire way. When she arrived, she jumped out of her car. No sign of break-in at her front door. She put the key in and turned it.

Everything looked normal. She walked into the kitchen and turned on the light. There, on the table, sat the laptop. She sucked in her breath, the hairs on her arms standing on end. Was someone in the house right now? Were they watching her? She looked around, training her ears for any sounds. Slowly, she walked toward the table and opened the laptop. It did look just like her boss'. But how would she ever swap them out? He always had his with him. He took it home at night and brought it with him to meetings, even to lunch. Probably the only time he didn't have it was when he went to the bathroom. And it wasn't like she could just run in and swap it out in front of Karen.

Hell.

Her belly twisted into tight knots just thinking about it.

Why did they want her to replace his laptop? Were they stealing company secrets? Or sabotaging something? Maybe inserting bad code into the security system or something? Getting his thumbprint swipe to unlock things?

She put the laptop in her satchel and sat at the table, too upset to eat anything. She chewed on her thumbnail. Well, she had all day to make the swap. She would think of something. But what if he didn't come into work for some reason? Or was in meetings all day with it?

She stood up and paced, imagining every possible scenario she could come up with. None of them were great. Midnight came and went. She couldn't even think about sleeping.

HE KNEW something was wrong the moment he woke up that morning. Shifter instincts are always spot on; the trouble is, he didn't always know how to decipher them. Like the night he'd met Ashley.

The sense grew stronger as he got off the elevator.

"Good morning, Mr. Stone," Karen said.

"Morning, Karen."

He walked to Ashley's office. The instinct had been about her last time. She didn't look up at first, which was odd for her.

"Good morning, Mr. Stone," she said when she

did. Her face was pale and she had circles under her eyes as if she hadn't slept.

"What's wrong?"

"Nothing," she said too quickly. "Just a bit of a headache. But it's not a migraine. I'm fine."

He smelled the acrid scent of fear. What was she afraid of?

Unable to think of what to say to get her to open up, he turned and walked away. This was one of those moments where he could have used charm lessons from his brother.

Their father had been rude and gruff like him, but Leon had possessed the gift. He could talk anyone into anything. Everyone liked him, and he'd made such a great leader. Ben, on the other hand, was a Class A Asswipe. And he led like their father had. Which is why he didn't want the responsibility of his brother's pack.

He left her alone for most of the day. By afternoon, though, he could sense her agitation through the walls. But it was none of his business. If she had something on her mind of a personal nature, he had no right to force it out of her. Still, it raised the protective instincts in him. He wanted to fix it, whatever it was.

He couldn't get anything done with Ashley fretting in the office next to him. It was one of the reasons he hated having anyone else working on the same floor as him. He hoped this didn't become a regular thing. By four in the afternoon, he picked up his laptop, ready to head out early for the day.

Ashley came barreling out of her office. "Are you leaving?" Her voice was three pitches higher than usual.

He stopped and turned slowly. "Yes, why?"

"Um, I, uh, wanted to go over some stuff with you. Can you stay for just a few more minutes?"

The smell of fear tingled in his nostrils. He scented desperation. What in the hell was up with her?

He turned back to his office and held out his arm with a bow, as if ushering her in.

She gave him a wan smile. "Thanks. I, uh, will be right there. I just have to grab my notes."

She returned with a stack of things, which she placed on her lap, rather than the top of the desk.

"Okay, you've been acting weird all day. What's going on?"

"Nothing," she said, rubbing the back of her neck. "It's just a headache, I swear."

Her eyes didn't meet his, but seemed to be looking at his briefcase. "Okay," she said, drawing a breath. "I just wanted to get your opinion on some ad ideas I have for the campaign."

He narrowed his eyes. "It couldn't wait till tomorrow?"

"I'm sorry," she exclaimed, standing up out of her chair and setting the stack of things on his desk.

"You're in a hurry? Let me just show you this one thing—" She pushed a notebook under his nose, and at the same time she lunged across his desk and knocked a cup of cold coffee all over him.

Anger surged. Without a doubt, she had done it on purpose. Why would she try to trick him? His blood turned cold. He leaped back, dripping as she ran around to his side of the desk. "Oh, my God, I'm so sorry. I will clean this up if you want to go to the restroom and get yourself dried off."

He smelled her sweat and fear even under the stench of coffee covering him. Reason won out over the instinct to pick her up by the throat and demand what was going on. He'd learn more watching her follow through on her game, whatever it may be. He walked out without a word.

He didn't go to the restroom, though. Karen was already up out of her desk, handing him a towel from the bar area where she served coffee or water to guests.

He kept his back to his office, watching from the corner of his eye as Ashley darted around and opened his briefcase. He couldn't see what she was doing, but he gave her enough time to finish it before he turned back. She was frantically wiping down surfaces when he came back in.

"I'm so sorry," she said. "I know you have to go. I shouldn't have kept you here."

"No, you shouldn't have," he said.

She didn't even notice the rebuke, a sign of her complete distraction. She gathered up her things and rushed back to her office. He saw his laptop poking out from under a piece of paper in the stack of things she carried.

He grit his teeth. What the hell had the little minx just done? And why? He shut the door to his office and closed the blinds. Setting the briefcase on his desk, he brought his nose down to it and sniffed. All he smelled was the damn coffee. He carefully opened the top of his briefcase and looked in. His laptop lay where he left it. At least it looked like his laptop. But was it a little shinier?

He sniffed. He detected a faint tar or pitch smell. Was it a bomb? Several seconds ticked by as he stared at it, assimilating that thought.

Why did Ashley want him dead? Or better yet, who had put her up to it? Was she a professional? No, she'd blundered the whole thing terribly. She definitely wasn't a pro. He wondered how much she'd been offered to commit murder.

Bitterness swelled in his chest. Betrayal coated his tongue, clung to his clothing and skin. He had trusted her, brought her into his inner circle of one. He should have known better. No one could be trusted.

He sat and stared at the laptop for a long time, wondering what to do with it. Calling the police did not even enter his list of possibilities. Shifters did not involve law enforcement. If anything, they tended to work on the fringe, outside of the normal boundaries of the law. He considered whether anyone in his brother's pack might help. Stanley, the new alpha, might know what you do when a bomb is left on your desktop. But he'd purposely kept his distance from the pack since Leon's death. He just needed to get the bomb someplace out in the open, where it wouldn't kill anyone when it went off. But what if it detonated before he disposed of it? His fingers tightened on his desk.

What was Ashley's plan? He should be trailing her. Damn, he needed help. Sighing, he picked up his cell phone and dialed Stanley.

"Ben," Stanley answered, sounding surprised. He'd been friendly enough, trying to get Ben into their fold although there had been subtle threats about the pack not liking lone wolves. As Ben was the largest and most ferocious wolf, Stanley had come out and said he would stand back if Ben wanted to be alpha—no challenge necessary. When Ben refused, Stanley had told him he expected his presence at their meetings, but he'd ignored the directive.

"Got anyone who can talk me through disabling a bomb?"

Stanley was silent a moment. "Mark Ruhl. He's our insider in law enforcement. He works for the DEA. You need help right now?"

"Yeah."

"Give me just a minute."

"Thanks."

He hung up. When the phone rang, he picked it up, even though he didn't recognize the number.

"This is Mark Ruhl. I hear you need some help?"

He exhaled. "Yeah. I believe there is an explosive in my laptop."

3

Ashley picked up her satchel with Ben Stone's laptop and stepped into the elevator. Her limbs dragged, weak from being so wound up for past twenty-four hours.

It's almost over. Then Melissa will be safe and you can go to the police and tell Mr. Stone what you've done.

She took the elevator to the third floor of the parking garage and got off. Clutching the satchel to her chest, she walked forward, toward the northwest corner. She had parked her car there that morning just to familiarize herself with the area. The cement walls echoed with her footsteps, the smell of exhaust and gasoline oppressive. The lot seemed empty—no other cars, no people, nothing. She stood and waited. Had she heard the time or place wrong? No, the words were still echoing in her mind. *Third floor, northwest corner of the lot.* She opened her car door and sat down on the seat with the door standing open. Sweat trickled down her ribs. She thought she heard a door close, but when she looked around, she only saw the stairwell door, and no one was near it.

Time ticked by. Five minutes, then ten.

God, she hoped Melissa was okay.

Suddenly, she heard the sound of a car coming up the ramp. She stood up and took the laptop out of the satchel, her hands clumsy. The satchel dropped to the ground and she left it, craning her neck to get a look at the car.

A dark blue sedan approached. It was old and junky. She didn't know what she'd expected, but it had definitely been something more impressive. A Humvee or something. She took a few steps forward to show herself.

The car stopped and three men got out. She tried to see in the darkened windows for another person. Where was Melissa? The men walked toward her. They were young men—scruffy-look-ing, with tattooed arms and piercings. They wore t-shirts and jeans and they palmed guns.

"Where's Melissa?" she called out.

"You got the laptop?" one of them asked as they drew closer.

"Maybe," she said, clutching it to her chest and backing toward her car. As if she had any chance of not giving it to them when they were armed and it was three against one. "Where's Melissa?"

"She's in the car. Give us the laptop and you can see her." They had backed her up to her car now, surrounding her.

"I want to see her first."

One of them cocked his gun and held it up to her temple, pushing hard against her skull. "Hand it over," he said as his friend grabbed it and tried to pry it from her chest.

"No," she said struggling.

The guy with the gun smacked her head with it and she fell back against the car. She lost her grip on the laptop and one of them snatched it away.

Another one grabbed her arm and yanked her forward. "You're coming with us, honey," he said.

A terrible snarl sounded from the other side of her car and suddenly a huge black animal leaped over the car, gleaming white teeth snapping. Its jaws closed over the neck of the man holding her and they both tumbled to the ground, the beast snarling and growling as they rolled together. Gunshots rang out from both directions, and the animal yelped and let go, but sprang to its feet, crouching to attack another man. The men continued to fire at the animal, the sound ricocheting around the concrete parking garage. Screaming blared in her ears—her own voice, she realized. The laptop had fallen to the ground and she grabbed it and took off running for their car. If her sister was in it, she needed to get to her.

The animal launched at her, knocking her down. She screamed, expecting it to move in for the kill, but instead it turned, lunging at one of the men.

"Let's go, let's get out of here," one of them yelled, helping up the most severely wounded and dragging him toward their car.

She climbed to her feet to follow, but the wolf—or whatever it was—turned and snarled, blood dripping from its muzzle. She took a step back. It snarled again, blocking her way, then it chased the remaining man, tackling him once, but then taking another gunshot wound that left it lying as the man jumped in the driver's seat and the car screeched off.

She ran a few steps after, then stopped, seeing the beast climb to its feet. She froze. It turned amber eyes on her and growled, low and menacing. It was covered in blood, and its fangs looked razor-sharp. It advanced.

She backed up slowly. "Easy, big guy," she said, her heart in her throat. She didn't make eye contact or any sudden movements. If she could just get to her car, she'd be all right. It continued to follow her, though, his head lowered, fangs bared. The growl was like nothing she'd ever heard before. Unworldly. Terrifying.

Her butt hit the car and she fumbled for the door, not wanting to turn her back on the animal.

The wolf stalked closer and she shrieked, scrambling up on the trunk to get away.

The beast suddenly transformed, growing taller, thinning out. She blinked, thinking she had lost her mind.

Ben Stone stood in front of her, dripping in blood, naked, and looking furious. He yanked open the back door to her car and pulled her off the trunk at the same time. "Get on the floor," he said, pointing to the back seat. "Head down, eyes lowered. *Now.*"

BEN SLAMMED the back door on Ashley's huddled form and climbed in the driver seat, where he found her keys on the front seat. He drove like a bat out of hell down to the first floor of the parking garage, stopping behind his car.

He had a hidden button for keyless entry to the trunk, just for occasions like these. He also kept a duffel bag with clothes, spare keys, a wallet with a second set of credit cards, cash and IDs, and other useful items inside. He grabbed the bag and yanked on a pair of jeans.

Pulling out a roll of duct tape, he stalked around to Ashley's car, where she had climbed out.

He grabbed her wrists and wound the tape around them while her eyes rolled around in her head with horror.

Dammit. He had a world of trouble on his hands now. Not only had he allowed his enemies to get away, he'd revealed himself to Ashley, who also belonged on his enemy list.

He caught his breath when he saw her entire side was covered in blood. Shoving her back onto the car seat, he yanked open her blouse. Her skin was blotched with the blood, but he saw no bullet hole or wound.

"Where are you hurt?" he demanded.

"I-I," she swallowed as if her mouth were dry. "I think it's your blood," she croaked.

He exhaled in relief and looked down at his own torso to survey the two gunshot wounds he'd taken. They would heal. He must have bled on her when he tackled her to stop her from going to their car.

He lifted Ashley's ankles and wrapped the duct tape around them, then ripped off a smaller piece for her mouth.

She twisted her head away when he came toward her with it, the whites of her eyes glowing. "Please," she panted, the metallic smell of fear coming off her in waves. "Please don't."

He hesitated.

Don't be soft. She's the enemy.

He pointed a finger in her face. "You make one sound and I'll put you in the trunk. Nod if you understand me."

She bobbed her head up and down.

He slammed the door on her and climbed back in her car, tossing his duffel bag onto the seat beside him. He needed to get out of there before real trouble showed up. Those pathetic boys weren't the brains behind the operation.

He knew Ashley wasn't the mastermind, either, or she wouldn't have been attacked by the men back there. Still, she had sold him out—and that bothered him more than any of the rest of it. Maybe, that first night when he met her, his instincts had gone off because she was a danger to him.

But no, that didn't feel right. It had been attraction, not danger.

He pulled a baseball cap down low over his eyes and took off, out of the parking garage. He got on the highway and drove several miles, weaving in and out of traffic and keeping his eyes glued to his rearview mirror. They didn't seem to have a tail. When he was sure of it, he took the next exit and pulled into a seedy motel on East Colfax—the kind that rented by the hour for cash and no ID.

He opened the back door and grabbed the duct tape again. He taped Ashley's hands to her feet, then wound the tape around the handle of the back seat.

"You make one sound, or you try to escape, and I will kill you. Nod your head if you understand."

She whimpered, panting for breath, but nodded.

"I will be right back. Don't move."

He slammed the door again and checked into a room. When he returned to the car, he cut her feet free and tossed a sweatshirt over her bound hands. "Let's go," he said, hauling her out of the car. "Not one sound out of you."

She looked around wildly, but didn't make a peep other than the sound of her breath rasping in her chest.

He took her into the room and used a length of rope to string her wrists up over the bathroom door. She stood on her tiptoes, swaying. Turning his back on her, he washed up, cleaning his gunshot wounds, which had nearly stopped bleeding. The bullets would come out in a few days. Shifters had incredible healing abilities. He rinsed his mouth out to rid the taste of blood and spit.

He was impressed that Ashley still hadn't made a sound. He'd expected some kind of noise by this point. He turned back to her, considering.

"All right, Ashley. I'm going to ask you some questions and you're going to answer." He fished in his duffel bag for his belt and pulled it out. Walking behind her, he unzipped her skirt and let it fall to the floor.

"Wh-what are you doing?" she asked, sidling as far away from him as her bound wrists would allow.

"Baring my target."

She whimpered, twisting and turning and looking up at the ropes binding her hands.

He ignored her antics and pulled her panties down just below her buttocks. He stood back to admire the view. He wasn't surprised to find her ass as perfect as he'd imagined it. Picking up the belt, he wound the buckle end around his fist.

Her eyes bulged. He caught her hips and turned her to face away from him. "I suggest you hold still," he warned just before he brought his belt down across her buttocks with a light slap to perfect his aim.

She shrieked, dancing away from him, her feet lifting from the floor and kicking in the air. His intention had been to intimidate her, and it seemed to be working, because he knew that hadn't really hurt her. He caught her wrists and pinned them against the door to hold her in place. He struck again, just a little harder.

She jumped as if shocked by electricity, her feet dancing to one side.

"Who hired you to kill me?" he demanded.

Noises came out of her, but they were incoherent sputtering.

He whipped her again. "I asked you a question," he growled. "Who hired you to kill me?"

A string of nonsense syllables erupted from her, tumbling from her mouth one after the next.

He considered. He'd wanted her scared, but having her too terrified to speak wouldn't work. Walking around the front of her, he pulled out his knife. Her eyes rolled back when he lifted the blade. He cut her down just as her eyelids fluttered and she fainted.

Damn.

He caught her limp form as it tumbled down and carried her to the bed where he sat with her cradled in his arms.

Within a few seconds her eyes opened and she blinked, looking up at his face.

He brushed the hair back from her big blue eyes and they looked at each other. Propping her up on his knee, he said, "Okay, we're going to try this again. I need answers from you and you're going to give them to me."

She immediately began to struggle, twisting in his arms as if to dive off his lap. He used it to his advantage, pulling her face down over his knees. Her panties were still tangled around her thighs. His hand slapped down on her bare ass with a satisfying smack. She had a perfect bottom for spanking—plump and round, muscled globes that led into shapely thighs.

He slapped one side, then the other, over and over again. He'd just wanted to make her talk without actually harming her, but as he spanked her, his anger over her betrayal ebbed, turning to sympathy as she kicked and wriggled and her beautiful ass turned rosy and then a darker shade of pink. He held her snugly against his body and took care not to slap too hard. Shifters had superhuman strength, and the idea of bruising or actually harming his little assistant didn't sit well with him. Even if she had tried to kill him.

"How much did you get paid for killing me?"

"I didn't—"

He spanked the back of her thigh, causing her to yelp and kick. "How much?"

"Ow… ah… I wasn't trying to kill you. All I had to do was take your laptop," she gasped in a rush.

"And leave the one with the explosives in it."

She went still for a moment, her head lifting.

His heart skipped a beat. She hadn't known about the bomb. Satisfaction warmed his blood. He rested his hand on her blazing cheeks.

"Who gave you the laptop?"

"I don't know."

He resumed spanking. "Who hired you?"

"No one hired me."

He spanked harder.

"Wait!" she cried. "It's true—no one hired me. They kidnapped my sister!"

He froze, his hand mid-air.

"They said they would bring her tonight, but she wasn't there." Ashley's voice sounded strangled.

ASHLEY ABRUPTLY FOUND herself lifted upright and plopped on Ben's knee, his green eyes boring through her.

"It's true," she whispered, seeing he was searching for something in her face.

"You should have come to me," he said, his voice hard like steel.

Her bottom throbbed, his jeans rough against her bare skin. She swallowed. "They said they'd kill her," she croaked.

He pursed his lips. The intensity with which he regarded her had an animal-like quality—as if he was a hunter and she his prey.

The memory of the huge wolf leaping over her car flashed in her mind. "What are you?" she whispered.

Abruptly, he stood, shoving her to her feet. "Go stand in the corner with your panties down," he said, pointing to the juncture of two walls, his expression dangerous.

She didn't even think of not obeying—he had

her so cowed, she would have dropped to her knees and licked his shoe if he'd ordered it.

She shuffled across the room, putting her nose in the corner, intensely aware of her bare ass on full display. She wondered how red it looked. Her cheeks felt hot and stingy and for some bizarre reason, her pussy pulsed in rhythm with the throb there.

"I'm stepping outside. Don't move, not even an inch from that corner. If you do, I will spank you again and this time it will be with my belt."

She shivered, but need made her dare to ask, "What if I have to pee?" She peeked over her shoulder at him.

His eyes narrowed. "Do you?"

"Yes."

"Go now, then," he said.

She walked toward the bathroom, grabbing one side of her panties with her bound hands and trying to pull them up.

"Leave them," he barked.

She looked over to find him trailing behind her toward the bathroom.

"What are you doing?"

"Keeping an eye on you." He leaned in the doorway to the bathroom and folded his arms across his chest.

She willed herself to stop blushing as she sat on the toilet and stared at a spot on the floor. When she finished, she wrestled with the toilet paper, the duct tape making it hard for her to wipe herself.

"Need some help?" he asked.

Was that the glimmer of a smirk on his lips? She glared at him. "No." She started to pull up her panties, then stopped, figuring he'd bark at her again.

"That's right," he said, motioning her forward. "Panties stay down until I pull them up."

She made a huffing sound and tried to walk without shuffling, back to the corner.

"Stay."

Woof. She didn't say it out loud.

Her boss was a werewolf. A huge, black, terrifying beast who somebody had tried to use her to kill. Why? And what would he do with her now?

She stood holding her breath as he left. Her bottom was on fire, and the humiliating position infuriated her, but she was very well aware of the fact that he hadn't hurt her. Well, other than her backside. Considering she'd just seen him trying to rip throats out with huge, sharp fangs, that said something.

The memory of him standing shirtless over her, tearing open her blouse and examining her with concern flitted before her eyes. Even though he thought she'd tried to kill him, he'd been checking her for injuries. He'd rescued her from those men, who had been trying to take her with them.

The motel door opened and closed and she sensed him behind her.

His thumbs hooked under the elastic of her panties, sending an electric shock where they touched her skin. Despite it all—despite her terror that he was going to kill her, despite the rather sound spanking he'd given her, despite the humiliation he'd just subjected her to, her body thrummed just to be near him.

He slowly drew her panties up, an act that seemed more intimate even than if they'd just had sex. Her pussy clenched.

"Good girl," he murmured, his breath hot in her ear. Her nipples puckered. Shivers of electric excitement ran through her body, but too soon, he stepped back. "Put on your skirt, we're leaving."

"Where are we going?" she asked, her knees weak as she tried to step into her skirt without falling.

"You're not in a position to ask questions," he said and gave her panty-clad bottom another slap.

"Am I your prisoner?"

He pulled the pillowcase off one of the pillows and used it to cover her bound wrists as he led her to the door. "Yeah. You're my prisoner." His voice was deep and gruff and it seemed to enter her body and send shockwaves from her core down her legs.

He led her to her car and opened the back door. "Get in."

She slid into the back seat. He immediately pushed her down to lie on the seat and taped her wrists to the base of the front seat, preventing her from sitting up. He leaned over her with the pillow-case open and she realized his intent.

"Wait, no," she shrieked as the case came down over her head.

The car door slammed.

"Mr. Stone," she cried. "Ben! Please. Please take it off." She struggled to dislodge it, rubbing her head against the seat.

The car started.

"Please. Please," she begged.

"Calm down, Ashley. I can't have you seeing where I'm taking you."

The car began to move.

"Get this off me. Get this fucking thing—" She thrashed around, yanking at her wrists to get them free. "Oh, God," she moaned when it seemed clear he wasn't going to take it off and she couldn't get it off on her own. "Oh, God."

Panic took over. She couldn't breathe. She screamed over and over again, drawing in short gasps of breath between shrieks. Her feet kicked at the door, her bound wrists thrashed so much she punched herself in the face.

The car swerved and braked hard.

Oh, crap, she'd made him mad. He was going

to put her in the trunk. She tried to stop screaming, but she couldn't get control.

The car door opened and the pillowcase came off with a whoosh. He reached for her and she cowered, thinking he would strike her. Instead his large hands grasped her head, cupping it, stilling her. His palms were over her ears, muffling her sense of sound. The forced quiet gave her a strange sense of security, as if she was cocooned safely by those hands, protected.

He was leaning over her, his brows drawn together with the same expression he'd worn when he thought she'd been hurt. Pained—like her panic attack had caused him pain. And he'd shrugged off his own bullet wounds. Which… what the hell had happened to them? He wasn't even bleeding anymore, nor did she see any sign of a bandage under his tight-fitting t-shirt.

"You're claustrophobic." It was a statement, rather than a question.

She nodded rapidly, still unable to catch her breath.

He began to fold the pillowcase lengthwise. She jerked away when he held it up to her head, but he persisted, wrapping it over her eyes like a blindfold. It wasn't long enough for him to tie in the back, though.

"I won't look. I'll lie down and I won't look, I promise," she promised, still shaking like a leaf.

He ignored her, pulling out the duct tape. Once more, he positioned the pillowcase over her eyes, then wrapped the duct tape all the way around her head, securing the fabric like a crown around her head. "There," he said. "Lie down."

A wedge of fresh fear shot up and she groped wildly for him, her fingers landing on his t-shirt, which she wrapped up in her fist. His heavy hand dropped onto her nape. He muttered a curse, then pulled her out of the car.

She panicked, twisting wildly in his grip. "Not the trunk. Please—not the trunk. I'll be good, I promise."

To her shock, he wrapped his arms around her and held her against his chest. He didn't say a word, but there was no mistaking the intended comfort. She clung to him, her body trembling against his hard muscled form. She drank in his strength, the solidity of his body. Inch by inch, her body relaxed.

"You're not going in the trunk," he said gruffly. "You're riding up front with me."

"Oh." She willed herself to stop shaking as she took a deep breath. He released her from the embrace and wrapped a firm arm around her waist, guiding her forward and around the car. He followed her head in with his hand as she sat, the way the cops do on crime shows. His weight pressed against her and she heard the click of her seatbelt.

Returning to the driver side, he climbed in. She

heard the rustle of movement, then he grasped her head and pulled her down until it connected with his thigh. He'd put something soft over the center console—a sweatshirt, maybe. She appreciated the thoughtfulness. "Stay down," he said, a note of warning in his voice.

She brought her bound wrists to his leg and wrapped her hands around it, as if he were her security blanket, and she just needed to feel his warmth to stay calm.

He put the car in gear and backed out, one hand still on her nape holding her down. Except then his hand began to move. His fingers threaded into her hair and closed into a fist, tugging slightly but not hurting her. They opened and closed again.

She held perfectly still, not wanting him to stop. She imagined his hands gripping other parts of her body, his touch rough, his grasp firm. What would it be like to be taken by him? Did werewolves have sex with humans? The image of him rolling with his opponent in wolf form, all snarls and teeth, returned to her.

What was he going to do with her? Maybe it was Stockholm syndrome, but she wanted to believe he would take care of her. That he wouldn't harm her.

But what about Melissa? She was someone's prisoner right now, too—if she was still alive. Had she been harmed? How had her captors treated her?

Ashley needed to escape Ben Stone and get to her sister with the laptop before it was too late. She needed to get her head back in the game and come up with a plan, right away.

BEN DIDN'T MEAN to make love to Ashley's hair with his hand, but once he'd buried his fingers in the glossy, thick mane, it became a compulsion. He stroked along the back of her head, twisting it up into fistfuls and releasing it. Damn, he wanted her.

He'd smelled her arousal when he'd put her in the corner. It had shocked him. He'd just scared her to the point of fainting and then spanked her until her ass turned rosy and she still wanted him? His cock stiffened at the thought. What about this human woman affected him so strongly?

She shifted her position, pulling her hands away from his leg and moving her feet. She was probably completely cramped in the position in which he'd put her. Her foot tangled with her purse where he'd thrown it on the passenger side floor.

It took him a moment to realize she was stealthily moving the bag closer to her. He watched, waiting to see what she was up to. She made another shuffling movement and used it to shove the bag up underneath her hands.

Bile rose in his throat, the wound from her earlier deception still raw. He willed his breathing to stay in control as she rolled her body forward, her face pressing into his leg. Her bound hands dropped into the bag, as if idly hanging there. When they emerged, she clutched her phone.

He pulled the car over to the side and threw it in park. In a swift motion, he hauled her torso further over his lap and whipped up her skirt.

"What do you think you're doing?" he demanded, snatching the phone from her hand. Yanking her panties into her crack, he landed several hard spanks on her sit spots with it. It was a stretch to reach her backside in the awkward position, but he managed it, punishing her already red bottom while she writhed and squirmed beneath him. She had a wide, thin phone and its plastic case made a satisfying thwap each time it connected with her rosy flesh. "Dammit, Ashley! Was the claustrophobia just a big ruse? Were you just tricking me to earn my sympathy?"

"No," she shrieked. "No, it wasn't a trick. Stop, please. Ouch!"

"I will stop when I have made my disgruntlement clear."

She wriggled over his lap as he continued to

spank her. "Ow, stop!" She sank her teeth into his left thigh.

Rather than anger him, it had the odd effect of making him want to throw her down and fuck her brains out. Female wolves bite and snarl while having sex, and she had just flipped a switch in him. His vision domed and his teeth sharpened with the need to mark her. He leaned his head back against the seat, closing his eyes and breathing deeply to regain control.

She didn't take the pause in spanking as a victory, huddled tense and still on his lap. "I'm sorry," she said in a small voice.

He didn't open his eyes. "Who were you going to call?" he asked in a tired voice.

"No one. I just need my phone… in case they call."

Irritation cut through his arousal, bringing him back to his rational self. "Did you think I wouldn't let you answer it? Setting up a new meeting is key to me figuring out who the hell is behind this."

Her little hands pawed at his jeans, plucking the fabric. "Sorry," she said in a small voice. "I didn't know." After a moment of silence, she said, "I was thinking I might text them."

"Blindfolded?"

"Well, getting the blindfold off was my next problem."

He made a growling sound. "What were you going to text?"

"Something like, *I still have the laptop and I want my sister.*"

He handed her the phone and pulled up the blindfold by an inch. "Go ahead."

She texted the words and showed him first before hitting send. He took the phone from her and put it in his pocket, then pushed the blindfold back in place. "You don't move without my permission, understand?"

"Yes, sir."

He sighed and started the car back up.

"What about my sister?"

"We'll find her," he said.

She pushed herself up, her elbow going into his erection.

"Ouch." He jerked and pulled her back down to the original position. "Stay."

"Woof."

He almost smiled at that. Damn, she really tweaked him. He let himself touch her hair again, telling himself it was only to move it out of her face. But that didn't make sense, since she couldn't see anyway. The silky strands slid between his fingers as he pulled back on the road and tried to ignore the sight of her ass, still on display and flossed with her panties. The smell of her arousal filled the car like aromatherapy for his already raging libido.

He pulled up at the old warehouse his brother's pack used as a meeting place. No other cars were there, but that didn't mean anything. Mark Ruhl had talked him through disarming the explosives on the phone, but he'd arranged to meet him here to give him the laptop so he could analyze it, and monitor when the signal was sent for it to detonate. While at the motel, he'd called Stanley and asked him to come to the meeting as well. He would need a ride back to Stone Tech to get his car and the laptop and he needed someone to watch Ashley while he went. It wouldn't be safe to bring her back to the scene.

He entered cautiously, scenting the air. Empty. He pulled off the pillowcase blindfold once they were inside. Pointing to an old couch against one wall, he said, "Sit."

She glared at him, but obeyed.

"Little girl," he said, "You need to stop giving me those dirty looks, or I will take you back over my knee for a reminder of who is in charge around here."

She wobbled on her feet, and he would swear the look she gave him was pure desire, but she looked hastily away.

"That's better," he said, his voice thicker than usual.

He lifted his head, catching a sound at the back door. It pushed open and Stanley and three other males strode in, naked. Shifters were unabashed about nudity, but for the first time, he found himself bothered, not liking the way Ashley stared at them. They grabbed clothes from their lockers, stalking over, eyeing her. He became acutely aware of how out of place she looked, still dressed in her narrow work skirt and heels, her blood-stained blouse gaping because he'd popped all the buttons off when he tore it open to check for injury. Why the hell hadn't he put her in his shirt first?

"Hey, Stanley," he said. "Hey, guys."

"Who's she?"

"You don't need to know," he said. To Ashley, he said, "Lower your eyes."

She obeyed him, although he could see she was alert and paying attention.

"You brought a human to our private location," Stanley stated the obvious, his eyes narrowed.

"She was blindfolded."

"She knows what we are." He folded his arms across his chest.

"I'll handle her."

"How?"

The general code was to kill outsiders who found out. He bristled. "It's my problem and I'll take care of it."

Stanley raised his brows, looking at Ashley dubiously. "She looks like trouble."

4

Ashley had abandoned lowering her eyes to glower at the man named Stanley.

"My problem, not yours," Ben said.

What had he meant when he said he'd handle her?

"Yeah? So why are we here, then?" the aggressive wolf asked.

Ben's jaw hardened. "Someone's trying to kill me. I just need a little backup while I figure out who's behind it."

Stanley looked at him. "You're calling in a lot of favors for someone who's not even a member of the pack."

He shrugged. "If you're not willing to help, I'll deal with it on my own."

Stanley scowled. "You've already involved us.

You brought a human into our den, and now she's seen our faces."

A low, unearthly growl emitted from Ben's throat, sending shivers up her spine.

Stanley beckoned with both hands. "You want to challenge me for alpha? Do it. We both know you'd win. But if you just want to waltz in and pull favors without giving back, no one is going to fall in step behind you."

Nothing changed in Ben's face, yet she could feel his frustration.

A car pulled up outside. No one moved, the two men—or wolves—eyeing each other, tension radiating between them.

The door swung open. "Hey, Ben," a middle-aged man with a shaved skull and a tight white t-shirt said as he walked in. Like the other wolves, he was stacked with muscles. In fact, they all looked like they stepped out of a fireman's calendar. Except maybe a little less wholesome than firemen. There was a grungy roughness to the men that made her nervous.

"Hey, Mark."

Ben continued to eye the other wolves as he shook hands with Mark. "Thanks for your help earlier."

"No problem," Mark said, looking from Ben to the pack leader and back again, most likely sensing the tension. "Do you have the explosives?"

A chill slithered through her body at the word *explosives*. She might have killed Ben. She couldn't really blame him for not trusting her, could she?

He shook his head. "Not yet. I ran into a little trouble on my way out. I was hoping you'd drive me over there."

"No problem."

"And you want us to watch the girl," Stanley said flatly.

"Yeah."

"Who is she?"

Ben folded his arms across his chest. "She's my assistant. She left the bomb."

Five pairs of cold eyes turned to her.

She shrank in her seat.

"She was blackmailed." Ben handed Stanley Ashley's phone. "This is her phone. If the men who blackmailed her call, she has to pick up. Otherwise, don't trust her with it." To her, he said, "You tell them you have the laptop and you want to make the trade. You don't know anything about the wolf. Got it?"

She nodded. "Yes, sir."

Ben looked at Stanley. "So, are you willing?"

The man nodded grudgingly. "Yeah. We'll watch her."

Ben touched her shoulder, sending a jolt of electric energy through her. "Behave yourself. I'll be back within the hour." He left with Mark.

She instantly noticed the absence of his powerful presence. Not only did the energy in the room change, but she experienced a pang of dismay, as if being separated from him unsettled her. She definitely had Stockholm syndrome.

The men pulled out folding chairs and opened them, sitting in a ring around her.

"So… you're all wolves?"

Their leader gave her a cold stare, then turned to the other men, pointedly ignoring her. "What do you think?"

"About Stone?" asked the man beside him with a pierced eyebrow. "I think you were right to question his loyalty. I mean, I came because you asked me, but if he had called… well, the only reason I'd come would be out of respect to Leon's memory. But that collateral is going to run out soon if all his little brother does is take."

"Well, technically this is the first favor he's pulled in the three years he's been here," a younger Asian man spoke up.

She didn't know why she felt so relieved to hear someone speak in Ben's defense. She definitely didn't understand the politics underfoot, but she was catching enough to put it together. They were a gang of some sort, and Leon, Ben's dead brother had been a part of them, but Ben wasn't.

"Yeah, but where's he been? Lone wolves are trouble, that's all I'm saying," muttered the guy with the pierced eyebrow. "You know how Arctic wolves handle lone wolves."

"No, how?" the Asian man asked.

"The pack hunts them down and kills them. I mean *canis lupine,* not shifters. But I'm saying we could take a page from their book."

The other men grunted in some form of assent.

She attempted conversation again. "You guys are a pack? And this is your clubhouse?" she asked, looking around. The warehouse was made of steel construction, like a giant barn. The floors were plywood, painted gray but covered in dark stains. Folding chairs and tables were stacked against one wall, and a row of lockers stood in the back. On one end it sported the features of any good man cave—a pool table, foosball, and dartboard. Otherwise, it was a big, empty space.

What did they do here?

Stanley flicked his gaze to her. "No one is talking to you."

Her stomach rumbled. She had skipped dinner because she'd been too keyed up about the meeting. Now it must be pushing nine o'clock.

"Wanna play pool?" the pierced eyebrow asked.

"Yeah, sure." Stanley got up and followed.

She was left with the young Asian and a huge hulk of a man, who the Asian man called Brian. They talked on and on about baseball statistics.

After what must have been forty-five minutes,

she pushed herself to her feet, determined to find the restroom to at least get herself some water to drink.

"Where do you think you're going?" Brian asked, pushing her back down.

"May I have some water?"

He frowned. "Yeah, I guess so. Don't move." Brian crossed the room to the door she had guessed to be the bathroom. When he returned, he had a plastic cup full of water and a roll of duct tape.

"Thank you," she said, taking the cup of water awkwardly between her bound hands and eyeing the duct tape. Her fears were confirmed when he crouched at her feet and wrapped her ankles in tape. "That's really not necessary," she said. "I wasn't going anywhere; I just didn't want to ask you to serve me."

"Finish up," he commanded, holding his hand out for the cup.

She tipped her head back and downed the rest, then handed it to him.

He ripped off a small piece of duct tape.

"Oh, hey," she exclaimed, trying to scoot down the sofa away from him. "That's not necessary. I'll keep qui—"

The tape slapped over her mouth. She screamed between closed lips and brought her bound feet up, right between his legs.

Brian grunted in pain and his hand shot out, catching her hard across the cheek with an open palm.

She gasped, but with her mouth closed, couldn't suck in enough air, her nostrils coming together and locking, which only made her suck harder until the outer rim of her vision started turning black and lights danced before her eyes.

Calm down. Exhale.

Tears ran out of her eyes, not from the pain of the slap, but from her body's response to not breathing. She managed to get some air out of her lungs and back in, but it didn't feel like enough. The assholes had already walked away, which was a relief, because she wouldn't have wanted them to see her cry. She closed her eyes and leaned her head back against the couch, schooling her heart rate to slow down.

You can breathe through your nose. You can breathe through your nose…

She didn't know how long she'd sat there like that before the door opened. She unglued her eyelids to see Ben striding over to her, his expression dark and furious. She shrank down, not wanting to be the object of his anger.

He peeled the tape off her mouth, which hurt like hell. She blinked to keep back the pathetic tears that had sprung up at her relief to have it off. Glowering, he put a finger on her chin and turned it, looking at her cheek, which still stung.

He stood up. "Who hit her?" he demanded.

The huge guy walked over and said without concern, "She kicked me in the nuts."

Ben emitted a snarl and tackled the man in a flash, rolling on the floor in a tangle of flying limbs and inhuman growls.

She heard herself shriek and held her bound hands to her mouth to shut herself up. The other men gathered around, seeming largely unconcerned. Actually, they looked excited, like this was a cock fight and they had money riding on the winner.

"Aren't you going to stop them?" she demanded, looking at Stanley, their leader.

He shrugged. "Not yet."

Ben's fist emerged and he slammed it into Brian's nose, sending blood spurting in all directions. As it leaked onto the floor, she realized, with a lurch of disgust, that all the dark stains on the plywood must be from blood.

The men continued to roll and tumble, punching, and… yes, biting, slamming each other's heads into the floor or against their own heads. Ben's eyes glowed yellow, and his teeth seemed longer than human teeth.

"All right, that's enough," Stanley cut in, still without any tone of urgency.

Brian obeyed his leader, lumbering up to his feet.

Ben had not surrendered, and he launched another attack, but the three wolves grabbed him and pinned his arms back. "Stanley said enough," the pierced eyebrow growled.

Ben stilled, but his muscles stood taut, face twisted in rage.

Stanley held up his hand in a signal for Ben to stand down. "She wasn't marked," he said mildly.

She wondered what the hell that meant.

Ben shook off the men holding his arms and stalked toward her. In a smooth motion, he tossed her from the couch up over his shoulder and walked toward the door.

"Yeah, you're welcome, asshole," Brian muttered.

Ben didn't stop or turn, he just walked out the door and out to her car, where he gently set her on the trunk.

He drew deep breaths to regain his temper. He hated himself for leaving Ashley to be mistreated like that. What had he been thinking? Those wolves were not his friends. They were not even his allies.

"Close your eyes," he muttered, realizing he

shouldn't have taken her out of there without the blindfold.

By some miracle, she complied. He grabbed the blindfold and duct tape from the front seat and wrapped it on. She was shaking, and her expression was shell-shocked. He wasn't sure if it was from fury or fear. Probably both. He knew he should apologize; hell, he should be begging for her forgiveness, but he couldn't, for the life of him, figure out what to say. There was no excuse for what just happened to her. And it was all his fault. He was supposed to be protecting her and he had done nothing but terrify and traumatize the woman.

Yes, she had left a bomb in his briefcase, but he couldn't really blame her for that, could he? She hadn't known what it was. And even if she had, it was natural she would choose her sister's life over his. It was stupid to believe she might have some kind of attachment after working for him for only a week.

So why did it still bother him so much?

He was the one with the irrational attachment. And it was one that had already caused her a world of trouble. If he hadn't asked Ashley to be his assistant, if he hadn't been seen driving to her house and picking her up, moving her up to his floor, welcoming her into his life, she wouldn't have been targeted as the best possible candidate to plant the bomb. Her sister would be safe right now, and she would be blissfully unaware of the wolf who couldn't get her out of his blood.

He cut the tape off her ankles and helped her into the car. Climbing in on his side, he buckled her seatbelt.

She lowered her torso to the center, but seemed to purposely avoid placing her head on his lap this time. He didn't blame her.

He put the car in gear and started driving. Despite how abysmally this meetup had gone, there was one more wolf who might be able to help them, and Mark Ruhl had given Ben his address. Unfortunately, the computer hacker Jeff Zolla had left Stanley's pack for the Boulder pack, which meant he may not be willing to do anything for Ben at all. He figured it was better to show up in person than to try to call. But first, he needed to stop and see his sister-in-law because he had a bad feeling about who was behind this attack.

When he'd driven five miles, he pulled the blindfold off Ashley. "You may sit up now."

She sat up, looking out her window and blinking at the streetlights. "So... what? You just roll around and pop people in the nose every time you get pissed off?"

He didn't know what to say, so he said nothing. Thinking again of what that asshole Brian had done to Ashley, he ground his teeth.

"I don't know what you were so mad about. It's not like they did anything different to me than you've already done. I mean, you brought me over in duct tape. So they put more on. And he slapped my face. Well, you've slapped my ass. More than once. I'm your prisoner here, right?"

Her words hit him like a punch in the gut. She was right. He had treated her just as badly. Did it make it all right because he cared about her? Or because he believed he had a right to punish her for trying to kill him?

Spanking females was part of their wolf culture, just like solving grievances physically between males. But it must have shocked Ashley to be spanked. He knew he hadn't harmed her. He'd been careful only to use it as a show of dominance, not to cause her lasting pain. And from her scent, he thought she found it exciting. But to think she felt as abused by him as she did by them made him sick to his stomach.

He was bad for her. Really bad. And while he had an obligation to save her sister and protect her from the men who may want to harm her, the selfish part of him didn't want it to be at the expense of forever losing her esteem.

He abruptly exited Sixth Avenue West and pulled in at a Motel 6. It wasn't safe to take her home, but he could at least set her free if that's what she wanted. She had her car and her phone.

He could shift and go on foot. He got out of the car and walked around to her side. He cut her hands free and helped her to stand.

"You're not my prisoner. If you want to do this on your own, I will stay out of it."

Her eyes widened and then narrowed. She folded her arms across her chest. "Fuck that, Stone. I'm not going anywhere without you."

The wolf in him heard the challenge like some kind of mating call. Mad force took over and he pushed her back against the car, crushing her lips with his own. She tasted of berry lip gloss, her lips impossibly soft. He buried his fingers in her silky brown hair, made a fist and pulled. He wasn't thinking, hadn't even known he meant to kiss her, but when her tongue responded, licking into his mouth and tangling with his, the urge to mark her came on like a freight train.

He ground his painfully hard cock against her flat belly. He kissed her as if he might devour her, her sweet lips opening to accept his thrusting tongue, her fingers reaching to clutch his shoulders.

His skin prickled with heat, his vision turned sharp, and his canines began to lengthen.

Jesus Christ. He was about to mark her right there in the parking lot.

But damn, if he lost control, it could be dangerous for her. Hell, he could even kill her. When a wolf had sex with a female, his canines lengthened and he sank his teeth into her neck or shoulder. Biting caused instant submission so the female relaxed and allowed his domination. In the case of mating, he left his permanent mark on her—breaking skin to permanently embed his scent in her epidermis.

With a human, he shuddered to think what might happen—he could hit her jugular, and the pain he would cause her would be unforgivable. Especially because humans didn't heal overnight like wolves did.

Get off her.

His body would not obey his mind. He pulled her head back and licked a line up her throat, nipping her neck. The act triggered the true instinct, and suddenly his teeth were out, fully extended.

He jerked back, twisting to the side to get her neck out of the line of his jaws as they snapped closed. He turned his back on her and started walking swiftly away, needing to put distance between their bodies. He drew in deep breaths of the cool September air, gazing up at the moon as if it might somehow help him find his way back to sanity.

"Ben?" she called out. Despite her tough guy act, he caught a note of vulnerability in her voice.

"I'm coming," he said, his voice deeper than normal. He walked a wide arc around the car, as his vision returned to human norm and his teeth receded. He hoped the tightness in his pants would soon ease, too. After a couple of circles around his bewildered employee and the car, he came back to the driver's seat, climbed in, and slammed the door without looking at Ashley.

She climbed in and buckled her seatbelt.

"I'm sorry," he said gruffly. "That won't happen again."

She turned her head and stared at him, her expression a blank mask. What the hell did she think about all this?

Her phone rang. She dived for her purse, batting the phone out so it came flying up toward her face. She caught it with shaking hands and turned it over, looking at the screen. "It's them," she whispered as if they might hear.

"Answer it."

"H-hello?"

"What happened?" the electronically altered male voice asked.

"Where's my sister?"

"Your sister's going to die if you don't bring that laptop to us. What was that animal at the meeting place?"

"I don't know—it came after me, too. It chased me into my car and I drove off without seeing where it went."

A silence followed. Then, "Who have you talked to?"

"No one! Not a soul. I still have the laptop and I want my sister."

"Be prepared to meet. We'll call you with the location."

"Wait—when? What time?"

"Tomorrow night."

The line clicked off.

She looked up at him and exhaled. "Well, it sounds like she's still alive."

Maybe. He wasn't too sure. The fact that they hadn't brought her sister out of the car made him think they had no intention of letting either woman walk away.

She plugged her phone into the car charger. He was grateful she had one that worked on both their phones. "Do you think I should call my parents? I mean… they should know they might never see their daughter again."

"No," he said, lacing his voice with authority. "That would only endanger your sister."

He half-expected resistance, but she just nodded. "Ben?"

He liked that she used his first name, even though it was impertinent. "Yeah?" He braced himself for another heavy question.

"I'm hungry."

His initial relief at this easy-to-solve problem

was overshadowed by guilt. He should have known she was starving. What kind of provider was he that he let his mate go hungry?

But no, she wasn't his mate, nor could she be. He needed to stop thinking of her that way.

"Are you okay with fast food?"

"I'd be okay with dog food at this point," she muttered.

He saw a sign for a cluster of fast-food restaurants and he took the exit and went into the drive-thru. With her blouse ripped and covered in blood, he couldn't very well bring her in anywhere.

He ordered their food and paid for it, handing her the bag and getting back on the highway.

She unwrapped her sandwich and took a huge bite. "Do you want me to open something for you?" she asked with her mouth full.

Despite all the tension between them, he couldn't help but find her cute. He experienced a flash of longing. This is what it would be like if Ashley was his girlfriend. Talking with their mouths full, laughing, comfortable with each other. He couldn't remember the last time he'd laughed with anyone. Definitely not since Leon and his father's death. Not since he'd betrayed his family and left them to die.

~

ASHLEY STUFFED HERSELF, eating too fast. She leaned back against the seat, suddenly exhausted. "Where are we going?"

"First to my sister-in-law's, then to see a guy who might be able to help."

"Like those guys back there?"

He gave her a dark look. "I made a mistake," he said. "I shouldn't have left you with them. I'm sorry."

For some reason, his apology hit her with a pang. She hadn't expected any concessions from him, and it was easier to steel herself against his dark allure when he was being a jerk. Still, she'd known he was sorry. He wouldn't have attacked that other guy if not. And while the display of violence had been somewhat nauseating, it also left her feeling more than vindicated.

"Listen, Ashley… I should have warned you before we went in. Never get mouthy or disre-spectful with a wolf. It's taken as a challenge to the power structure, and swift, physical retaliation will always follow to re-establish order."

"Is that why you spank me?"

"Yes."

"You enjoy it, don't you?"

His eyes slid sideways, the corners of his mouth turning up. "I might enjoy some of it, yeah."

She flushed, two parts angry and one part something else. Something slithery and fluttery that moved in her belly. "Heathen," she muttered, moving her attention out the window.

"Ashley," he said, looking serious. "I mean it— don't offend anyone else. I know Brian asked for it, but this is important. If one of them had left a serious mark on you, I might have killed him. And then I'd have the whole pack coming after me, and consequently you. So it's a big deal."

I might have killed him. That piece of information made her slightly lightheaded. He did have a thing for her. She knew it.

"Okay."

"Yes, sir," he corrected.

"Yes, sir," she said, only slightly sarcastically.

"Thank you," he said.

She considered how much their relationship had changed in less than twenty-four hours. If it didn't go forward, could they go back? Working at Stone Tech seemed like a completely different world now.

"Ben?" She didn't know when she'd started calling him that. But considering she'd seen him naked and in wolf form, and he'd spanked her with her panties down, Mr. Stone didn't seem right anymore. "Do you mind when I call you that?"

She glanced at his chiseled face, the stubble growing on his jaw making him even sexier than when he was clean-shaven.

"No."

Would the man ever give more than the monosyllabic answer? His little speech about being respectful to wolves might be the longest he'd uttered.

"Do you think we'll ever return to work?"

"Yes."

"I mean… will I still be your assistant?" She held her breath. She wouldn't blame the man for firing her. After all, she had stolen from him and planted a bomb that could have killed him.

"Yeah," he said, but his throat sounded tight, as if he might be lying. Did he plan to fire her? Or worse… kill her? He had told the pack members that he would 'take care of' the fact that she knew about them. Was he just keeping her alive to arrange the meetup with the men who wanted him dead? Did he plan to kill her when it was all over? From what she could tell, he was a dangerous man.

"Will you still spank me if I get out of line?" she asked, trying to lighten her own tension, if not his.

It worked. Ben's shadow-smile appeared, that little hint of amusement that crinkled his eyes and touched the corners of his lips. "You like talking about getting spanked," he said.

Her pussy clenched involuntarily at his words. She held her breath, trying to ward off the blush she felt creeping up her neck. She plowed forward, though. "Who else have you spanked? Have you spanked Karen?"

"No," he said, sounding surprised. "Don't be ridiculous."

"Then who? Your girlfriends? Lovers? Were they wolves?"

"You were my first," he said.

Why did that answer please her so much?

"You were my first, too," she said, knowing she sounded like a little fool.

He actually smiled, which made her heart do strange things in her chest.

"So spanking is a wolf thing?"

He shrugged in the dark car. "It's a common practice. It's an easy show of dominance without causing any harm."

"So basically wolves are sexist pigs who think they're better than women and deserve to spank them?" She held her breath, expecting his irritation, but he smiled.

"No. I think some relationships fall more equally. But I'm a natural alpha. I don't think I'm better than women. I just need to be on top."

She considered that, remembering the words that had been tossed around at the warehouse. "I thought they said you weren't alpha."

It took him so long to answer she'd given up hope of a response, but at last he said, "I refused to lead my brother's pack. I just didn't have it in me."

She reached over and touched his thigh. "Well, of course it was too much. You already had to take over at Stone and you were probably still grieving his death to boot."

Ben's eyes shot over to her, a muscle jumping in his cheek. He looked slightly alarmed, as if shocked she understood him. At least she hoped she'd understood him. But he picked up her hand and moved it from his leg, which made her want to crawl under her seat for the rest of the drive.

Why couldn't she touch his leg when he'd just mashed her against the car and kissed the living daylights out of her? She slumped back in her seat and stared at the headlights of the cars passing them. Too much had happened that day for her to even try to make sense of it all.

HE PULLED into his brother's circular drive in Golden, a western suburb of Denver. Nestled at the foot of the Rocky Mountains, Leon's back yard featured spectacular views and even a natural, rocky mountain spring-fed creek running through. Motion-sensing lights went off, lighting the sidewalk.

"Am I coming in?" Ashley asked as he opened his car door.

"Yeah."

She climbed out and smoothed her rumpled skirt, holding her blouse closed.

He rang the bell.

After a long time, Shayla spoke from behind the closed door. "Ben?"

"Yeah, it's me. Sorry it's so late, but I have to talk to you."

She opened the door, her face tight, but she offered her cheeks for South American-style kisses. A female alpha, Shayla might be petite in human form, but was large, sleek, and fast as a wolf, with tan fur and yellow eyes.

"This is Ashley Bell. She's my assistant at Stone."

Shayla gaped at Ashley's torn and bloody blouse. "What happened?"

"May we come in?"

"Oh, of course, I'm sorry," she said, standing back to let them in. "What's going on, Ben?"

He rubbed his face. He knew Shayla didn't appreciate having drama dumped at her doorstep in the middle of the night when she had two kids asleep in their beds. Leon had been a perfect husband to her—providing her the lifestyle she wanted to be a stay-at-home mother. When he'd asked Ben to be their godfather, he'd made it clear that if anything happened to him, Ben's top priority was to run Stone Tech to provide the same luxury and comfort his family had grown accustomed to.

He also knew Shayla didn't necessarily approve of him and the way he'd handled things since

Leon's death. He could practically feel the judgment rolling off her in waves right now, and unfortunately, he probably deserved it all. God, did she know it was his fault Leon was dead? He hadn't been able to look her in the eye since the day they buried the mangled remains of his brother's body, which had been flown back to the States for the funeral.

"So why are you here?"

"May I sit?" he asked pointedly, although it was rude of him to highlight her lack of graciousness, considering he was the one crashing down her door when her kids were already in bed.

She blushed as he knew she would, and gestured toward the table. "Would you like something to drink? Some tea, maybe?"

He looked at Ashley.

"No, thank you," she said, "but you wouldn't have a shirt I could borrow, would you?"

He cursed inwardly. He should have asked Shayla for clothes for Ashley. What the hell was wrong with him? He should be more thoughtful about his woman's needs.

"Of course," Shayla said and disappeared into her room, returning with a small, mauve t-shirt, which looked almost child-size. She handed it to Ashley. "I hope this will fit," his petite sister-in-law said.

Ashley unfolded it and held it up to her chest.

"Thanks," she said. "Is there a restroom I could use to clean up?"

"I'll show her," he said, trying to redeem himself. He led her to the hall bathroom and ushered her in, shutting the door behind him.

She turned to face him. "You don't trust me?"

He didn't sense any hurt from her, just a question at face value. "I don't trust my own judgment where you're concerned," he said, stepping forward and unbuttoning the only remaining button on her blouse, the one between her breasts. The blouse fell open and he went dizzy at the sight of her lacy purple bra. It matched the panties he'd seen earlier. Her perky breasts filled it completely, flesh pushing forward out of its confines.

His cock thickened, pressing against his jeans zipper.

To his surprise, her small hands appeared inside his shirt, sliding up his abdomen, shoving up the fabric.

He sucked in his breath at the shock of her skin against his. "What are you doing?" he croaked.

"Didn't you get shot tonight?" she asked, pulling the shirt higher to examine him.

"Oh, yeah," he said, blinking to steady himself, He twisted to look in the mirror. The bullets had risen to the surface, ready to come out. He squeezed one of the wounds and it popped out.

Ashley caught it, turning it over in her fingers in awe. He repeated the action with the other.

"Shifters heal fast."

"So I see," she said, dropping the bullets on the counter and bringing her palms back to his torso. Everywhere she touched created a fire under his skin, his self-control ebbing with each passing second.

"Don't," he said, covering her hands with his own and pulling them away from him. This time, it was his hands that shook.

"Why not?" she asked, her voice husky.

"I'm losing control," he said, picking up the shirt Shayla had given her and pulling it over her head.

She slid her arms through the holes and pulled the shirt down. It was too small—the fit was skin-tight, showcasing her perky breasts and flat tummy, making her look like a Playboy bunny. He couldn't stay locked in the bathroom with her a moment longer. He turned and walked out, no longer concerned about what she might do in there. He vaguely heard the sound of running water as he walked away, trying to clear his head.

Shayla had put the teakettle on, despite their refusal of her offer, and was preparing the tea when he returned to the kitchen. He filled Shayla in on the evening's events, glossing over Ashley's part in the plot.

"Did you call Stanley?" Shayla asked tightly.

He blew out his breath. "Yeah. Mark Ruhl helped me with the bomb and Stanley and some guys met me at headquarters, but Stanley wasn't thrilled about me asking for favors."

Shayla traced a line on the table. "He never wanted to lead the pack," she said without lifting her eyes.

He heard the blame in her voice.

"He only stepped up to keep the Boulder pack from taking over, and already, their alpha Bruce is poaching all our members who are dissatisfied with weak leadership."

"You think my leadership would be any less weak?" he snapped, then immediately regretted it. It wasn't her fault he didn't have the balls to do what he'd been expected to do. "Never mind, forget I asked."

"Why are you here, Ben?"

He rubbed his eyes. "I have a suspicion who's behind this."

Ashley appeared in the doorway, eyes wide.

"Who?" Shayla asked.

"Well, one person knew about Ashley's new role and that she'd have the opportunity to switch out my laptop. And that same person would know the importance of what's encoded on the laptop."

"Jack."

"Yeah."

Ben had come to Shayla, because if it was Jack, he needed to know how much affection she had for the man who had been her husband's best friend and business partner.

She seemed to understand because she said, "Do what you need to do," in a hard voice.

He raised his eyebrows. "Are you sure?"

She nodded once, decisively. "If Leon had trusted him, he would've left the running of Stone to him. After all, Jack knew everything there is to know about it and he's been there from the ground up. Why would he choose you? I mean, yes, you have a business degree from Harvard, but you'd never even worked for him."

And he'd been gallivanting around like a party boy while Leon had worked his ass off to build a multi-million dollar company.

She left that part unsaid, but even so, it lay between them, along with all his other failures to meet his brother's expectations. The teapot whistled and Shayla and Ashley had some conversation about which kind of tea she preferred while he wallowed in a moment of self-hatred.

"Mama?"

He whirled to see his little niece padding in her footed pajamas. "Ellie," he said, jumping from his chair and swinging her up into his arms.

"*Tío,*" she exclaimed, wrapping her tiny arms around his neck in a strangling hold.

He pretended to eat her neck, making chomping sounds.

She squealed in delight. "What are you doing here?"

"Well, I came to make sure you were in bed. What are you doing out of bed, young lady?"

She laughed, not taking his mock sternness seriously for a minute. "You woke me up," she said.

"I'm sorry, *mi amor*. I'll tell you what—how about if I read you a story and put you back to bed?"

"No," the four-year-old said stubbornly. "I want to stay up with you."

"Well, I'm not staying, *angelita*. I just came to ask your mommy something and now I'm leaving. What do you say, want that book?"

The child looked indecisive. "Did you bring your girlfriend?" she asked, changing the subject and staring at Ashley.

He ought to tell her Ashley was his employee, not his girlfriend. But the idea of having Ashley really being his mate, having her at his side at family functions, the way Shayla had been Leon's, hit him with such a stroke of longing that he just wanted to pretend, even if it was only for a moment. "This is Ashley, *muñeca*. *Es muy bonita, verdad?*"

Ellie giggled. "*Tío* has a girlfriend, *Tío* has a girlfriend!" she chanted.

"*Ya, mi amor.* Let's get you to bed."

"No," she squealed, kicking her feet.

"I'll take her," Shayla interrupted, reaching for his niece. "You should probably go."

"I'm sorry," he said to Shayla as Ashley sprang to her feet.

"It's fine," she said in a voice that really meant it wasn't. "I think you should talk to Stanley again."

He didn't answer. He had a whole heap of shoulds hanging over his head as it was.

5

Zolla's house was dark and quiet. Ben knocked on the door, but no one answered and his wolf senses didn't detect anyone inside. He sighed and called the phone number Mark had given him for the omega. An omega was the lowest ranking in a wolf pack, usually because of size or some other weakness.

Zolla answered the phone by saying, "Ben Stone," with a note of surprise. Obviously he had Ben's phone number programmed into his phone, which would seem odd, except that the wolf was the kind of guy who was all about information.

"Hey, are you around? I was wondering if I could meet with you tonight."

"Oh, yeah? I'm not home right now, I'm at El Parador, the salsa club on Speer."

"I'll meet you there in twenty minutes." He hung up and ushered Ashley back to her car.

"Now where are we going?" she asked.

"Salsa dancing."

"Really?"

He didn't answer.

"Wait… really?" she repeated. "Are you serious?"

"Well, we're going to a salsa joint."

"Do you know how to salsa? Well, of course you do, you're from South America. You probably were born dancing."

"Pretty much," he said. In Latin America, every party had dancing, even the most simple get-togethers. He hadn't meant they would actually be dancing, but she seemed so stunned by it, he found himself asking, "Do you?"

"Um, not exactly, but I'd really like to learn. Will you teach me?"

His skin prickled at the thought of holding her close to him on the dance floor. It would be too much. But he couldn't make himself say no to her —she looked so cute looking over at him with pleading eyes. "We'll see," he said.

They arrived at El Parador and went inside. Ashley tugged at her too short t-shirt, looking embarrassed.

"You look fine," he said. In fact, she looked smoking hot. Still in her tight little work skirt and high heels, the t-shirt took away the business look of the outfit, leaving pure feminine pizzazz.

A band was playing on the stage and people were out on the dance floor. Tables were scattered around the perimeter and couples sat together, heads inclined toward each other. He didn't see any sign of Zolla.

He swept the room again, stopping short when he realized the omega was playing conga drums in the band. Zolla lifted his chin in greeting. Ben picked a table and sat down, ordering them drinks in Spanish.

When the song ended, Zolla appeared at their table. He wore a faded t-shirt with what looked like a coffee stain on the front. His hair needed cutting, hanging in his eyes and curling over his ears. He looked from one to the other of them.

Ben waved him into a chair.

"Okay, why are you here?"

"I need your help," Ben said.

"I'm not in your pack anymore."

"I don't have a pack. Someone's trying to kill me and they kidnapped Ashley's sister. I'm hoping you can trace a call and a license plate."

Zolla's eyes turned to Ashley, naturally dropping to her tight shirt.

He tensed. "Don't look at her," he said, trying to keep the menace he felt from his voice.

Zolla's eyes immediately lowered submissively. He held out his hand. "Gimme the phone."

Ben nodded to Ashley, who dug it out of her purse and handed it to him.

Zolla started scrolling through the screens. He was an omega because of his size. In human form, he stood at five-eight, tops, and while his body was all lean muscle, he was scrawny. As a wolf, he was the size of a canine, while most shifters stood at least half again as tall as an ordinary wolf. He freelanced as a computer programmer, and specialized in security, which made him an excellent hacker. He had set up the internal security software at Stone under Leon's direction.

Ben didn't know Zolla well, but he had a distinct memory of his brother praising him in front of the whole pack for removing the tracking devices from all their phones and providing other technology help to the pack. Leon had been good about signaling out individuals' achievements, showing his appreciation where all could hear and see it.

A heavy stone sank in his gut as he realized he had done none of that since he'd taken over Leon's company. No wonder the managers had lost interest in achievement. Had this been what Ashley had been trying to help him do by including people in meetings? Giving them buy-in and empowering them? He stabbed his fingers through his hair. God, he was awful at all of this. Having a dominant personality didn't make him a decent leader. In fact, he'd been the worst kind. He'd been like his father —a dictator. Well, at least he hadn't tried to lead the pack, or he would've run them into the ground, too.

"This phone was tappable and traceable," Zolla announced.

"Yeah, I figured. Can you clean it up?"

"Not if you want me to be able to trace calls that come into it."

"Oh, right. So can you? Trace incoming calls?"

"I can try, yes. Not from here, but from home," he said, without looking up. "And it depends on if they've removed their location software."

He exhaled. "Great, thanks." Writing down the license number he'd memorized from the car in the parking lot, he slid the paper across to Zolla. "This is the license plate."

Zolla nodded. "That will be easy to trace."

"Thanks."

Zolla looked at him speculatively. "So what happens to me if it's Bruce, my new alpha, who's trying to kill you?"

Ben's eyebrows shot up. "Why would he want me dead?"

"Come on, Stone. A lone wolf who's alpha material? Every pack leader around will be thinking you're angling to steal his pack. Maybe it's Stanley, have you thought of that?"

"It's not Stanley. And I'm not interested in stealing any pack."

"I know that, but what if Bruce thinks you are? What if I'm acting against him by helping you right now? Are you going to have my back?"

Ashley was listening intently. Zolla's eyes went to her and Ben growled.

The omega dropped his eyes again. "You should really mark her if you're that territorial."

"Consider what you just said to me and tell me that's a good idea," he said.

Zolla looked thoughtful and then nodded. "I see."

A wolf didn't put his mate into danger, and Ben was a walking target. If he even set foot in Venezuela again, he had no doubt he'd be marked for death by Sandoval, the pack leader and drug tycoon who took down his father's pack. And here in the States, someone had already ordered his death. Whether they were human or shifter didn't matter. He wasn't about to tangle Ashley in it any more than she already was.

"Well, we're back to my original question, then," Zolla said, levelling him as much of a challenging look as subordinate wolf would dare.

Ben blew out his breath. He didn't want to be responsible for anyone. He could barely handle his own screwed-up life, and now he had Ashley to protect and deliver from evil, too. He definitely didn't need anyone else on his tab. But what choice did he have?

"Yeah, I'll protect you."

Zolla grinned. "Pack of two, then."

He raised his eyebrows. "You're leaving your pack to follow me? You must be nuts."

"Nah. I've always known you were my pack leader. I've just been waiting for you to come around."

A strange sensation ran through Ben's body—a shudder of something—recognition? Acceptance of his fate? He didn't know. He swallowed the lump forming in his throat. "Thanks," he said.

Zolla nodded. "I'll search the data from the phone and keep tabs on future calls. Do you two want to stay at my place tonight?"

He looked at Ashley. No way was he letting her spend the night anywhere near another wolf. "Nah, I'll go find a motel nearby. Thanks for your help. You have my cell number, right?"

"Yep. You should stay a while—we're about to play another set."

"No," he said, and then hesitated when he realized Ashley was giving him puppy eyes. He shrugged. "We might stay for a dance or two," he said, wondering what had come over him.

Zolla grinned, not missing any nuance. "Enjoy."

Ashley beamed at Zolla as he departed and Ben had to bite back the territorial snarl in his throat.

~

Her insides melted like hot butter just thinking about dancing with Ben. Somehow she'd never pictured Stone Man as a smooth dancer, but she'd never pictured him as a giant werewolf, either.

Mr. Macho had ordered drinks and tapas from the waiter in Spanish without asking what she'd like, but she hadn't minded—she enjoyed the sound of the r's rolling off his tongue, the sexy lilt to his voice in a language foreign to her. And the sangria and little plates of food the waiter brought were delicious.

"Are you going to teach me how to dance?"

His lips twisted into that faint glimmer of humor she'd come to relish. He stood up. "Yeah."

She rose and he reached for her hand, his eyes skimming over her breasts, which she knew looked huge in the too-tight shirt. She glanced down and realized her erect nipples were poking through her bra and the shirt. *Great.* She flushed, then lost her breath at the way his eyes devoured her as he led her to the dance floor. Before she could think of anything to say, he spun her to face him, holding their clasped hands high and resting his other hand on the back of her ribs. His touch was light, but he controlled her body, propelling her forward and backward in a series of steps she didn't know.

She looked down, trying to watch his feet to figure out what to do.

"Don't. Just follow my lead." He twirled her out, stopped her, brought her back in. He sent her away from him and toward him, then pulled her close and moved his hips against her body. "You don't need to know anything. Give yourself to me."

Her knees nearly buckled. *Gladly.* She loved being moved through space by his confident guidance. She let go of her desire to get it right and trusted in his ability to lead. It was too fast for her to think, even if she'd tried.

He looked even more devastatingly handsome on the dance floor. He had a relaxed demeanor, his upper body appearing at ease as his feet moved swiftly beneath him. Even his face, usually set in such stony lines, relaxed, that hint of amusement in his gaze. Her panties were wet with arousal and for some reason, she had a feeling he knew it.

They danced for three songs, until she grew lightheaded with exhilaration. Then he leaned his head down toward her ear, making every nerve in her body alert with possibility. "We should go," he said, his breath hot in her ear.

Guilt stabbed her conscience. She shouldn't be enjoying herself while Melissa's life was in danger. She nodded and he led her to their table, where he dropped several twenties.

"I'll be right back," he said. He started to walk

away, then turned back. "You may *not* dance with anyone else," he said.

She raised her eyebrows, secretly pleased with his possessiveness, but not wanting to show it. "And what if I do?"

Leaning forward so no one would hear, he said, "I will take my belt to that beautiful ass again."

Her tummy flipped and her eyes shot to his face, trying to determine whether he was serious. His lips had a slight upward angle to them, a smirk of sorts, which probably meant he was serious but would enjoy it.

Why did that excite her so much? It really shouldn't. Something was definitely off with her. Instead of making her feel weak or cowed, his dominance and possessiveness thrilled her. She relished his attention. If only she could figure out how to lift the darkness that plagued him and crack his stony exterior.

He walked toward the stage and said something to the wolf who had promised to help trace her calls. When he returned, he took her hand—as if he was her boyfriend, not her boss—and led her out to the car. Except he didn't open the door for her.

Instead, he shoved her up against the body of the car, pressing his cock against her back, wrapping a fist in her hair. And then, he did… nothing. He appeared to be frozen in indecision.

"Grandmother… what a big… cock you have," she said, hoping to encourage him.

For a long moment he said nothing, his muscles as hard and tense as steel, pressing against her body, his breath a whisper at her neck. "All the better to fuck you with," he rasped after an eternity. He spun her around and started to yank her t-shirt off.

She held her arms against her sides to prevent it. She wanted him, but not in public, against the car. "Ben," she protested, struggling against him.

The shock in her tone seemed to change his eye color from gold back to green. He released her and jerked back, creating space between their bodies. Swearing softly, he stabbed his fingers through his hair. "I'm sorry," he muttered. He walked to his side of the car, and she felt the loss of his proximity in every cell of her body.

6

For the second time that night, he checked them into a low-budget motel, and purchased tooth-brushes and toothpaste from the reception desk.

After the past twenty-four hours of anxiety and fear, she should want only to crawl in bed and crash, but that was the last thing on her mind. She wanted Ben. Her body was on fire, and he just might be able to distract her from her worry over Melissa. She knew he desired her. She'd seen the hunger in his eyes, felt the tremble in his hands when she touched him.

I'm losing control, he had said.

She wanted to be the subject of that loss of control. She wanted to drown in those intense green eyes, see the flash of yellow when his animal side came out. She wanted him to hold her down and have his savage way with her—whatever way that may be.

She brushed her teeth in the bathroom and removed her skirt, hoping she made an alluring sight in the tight t-shirt and panties. She brushed her hair and applied lip gloss and she walked out of the bathroom with intention.

Ben was sitting on the edge of the bed and he did a double-take when he caught sight of her, but as usual, showed no emotion on his face. He stared as she walked to him and stepped between his legs, placing her panty-clad pussy right in his view.

He didn't touch her. "Go to bed, Ashley," he said, sounding tired.

Determination made her brave. "Fuck you," she ventured.

In less than a second she found herself pinned to the bed by a solid hand at her nape, and her panties down. Ben hadn't even moved from his place, he simply twisted in his seat to hold her captive.

"I think you must want another spanking," he said.

"Yes," she panted.

She heard him suck in his breath. He didn't move. He didn't lessen the grip on the back of her neck, but he didn't spank her either.

She remained perfectly still.

Then his palm fell on her ass, fast and furious.

She tried to keep still, since she had asked for it, but that only lasted a few moments before the sting set in. Then she wriggled and bucked, twisted and clenched to dodge the punishing blows.

She bit her lips to keep from crying out. She didn't want him to stop. She wanted it all—everything he had to give. Her bottom warmed under his hand, the initial sting fading after twenty or so spanks, turning into a delicious burn as he continued. It hurt, but it also felt good. She craved each stinging slap as it fell on her bare ass. She offered herself up to him, surrendered to his dominance. A pulsing heat grew in her sex, fueling the coil of need within her.

Abruptly, he stopped and released her.

She waited in tingling anticipation, opening her legs wider in a clear invitation.

"Go to bed," he repeated.

It felt like cold water thrown in her face. For a moment, she couldn't breathe, the indignity of being spanked and sent to bed too much. But desire made her bold. She scrambled off the bed and climbed over him, straddling his waist and pushing her breasts in his face.

His face twisted, as if in pain. "Don't," he grated. Yet one of his hands was already crushing her breast, the other kneading her ass. His grip was bruising, demanding, almost painful. She smashed her body against his, wanting more. His hot mouth landed on her hardened nipple, biting through her bra. Both nipples tightened, tingling for his touch. Her pussy clenched in eager spasms.

He shifted his grip, clamping one arm around her waist and reaching for her pussy with his free hand, rubbing over the silk gusset of her panties.

She lurched at the shock of contact with her most sensitive area, but he held her in place, his fingers slipping inside to slide roughly along her weeping slit.

"Ben," she groaned.

He dipped two fingers inside her and at the same time, shoved her t-shirt up and yanked it off her with one hand. As his fingers twisted and thrust inside her, he yanked down one side of her bra. His lips fell on her nipple, teeth grazed, tongue flicked as he tugged the bra down to her waist.

Her fingers fumbled with the clasp and she tossed it to the floor.

He thrust his fingers inside her again, hitting her g-spot and making her legs lose all strength. If he hadn't been holding her up, she would have collapsed to the floor. But he didn't slow down; he kept finger-fucking her until he had her dancing on his lap, the penetration sending her hips into fantastic gyrations. His cock bulged in his jeans beneath her, impressive in size. She wrapped her arms around his neck, clinging to him for stability as he made her squirm with overpowering need.

Just as she was about to come, he withdrew his fingers, still wet from her juices, and pressed one against her anus.

She jerked, trying to hide it from him. He held her fast, pushing insistently as his other hand came from the front. He shoved two fingers—oh, God, was that three?—inside her pussy, as one digit breached her back hole.

She bit into his shirt and screamed through closed teeth, holding still.

No one had touched her back hole before. *Mess with the bull, you get the horns.* Ashley had known Ben Stone would be intense, but she hadn't expected things to go this way, this fast.

He alternated penetration—first thrusting into her pussy, then her ass, filling her, stretching her, sending her over the edge. Her eyes rolled back in her head, she mewled and yowled like a cat in heat, completely out of control.

The sensations cascaded through her—pussy, clit, and anus all hit with stimulation at once. She arched, shoving her breast against his mouth. The moment he sucked her nipple back into his mouth with a hard pull, she came apart. Throwing her head back, her body bucked on its own accord when the climax began to rock through her. The room spun and her skin burned, scorched in every place Ben Stone touched her.

Before she'd caught her breath, her reality

tipped and she found herself on the bed, with Ben easing his fingers out of her. His face held none of the relaxation she experienced, his eyebrows drawn together in pain. He leaned over and kissed the apex of her nether lips with reverence before disengaging and walking to the bathroom.

She lay there, staring at the ceiling, her heart still galloping as she enjoyed the bliss. She thought Ben would return, perhaps with a condom, but she heard the sound of the shower turning on.

Kicking off her panties, which were now tangled around her ankles, she padded to the bathroom and pushed open the door.

The shower curtain stood open and Ben leaned against the tile wall of the stall, eyes closed, his fist closed around the largest cock she'd ever seen. The muscles in his sculpted chest and arm rippled as he pumped his manhood with an urgency that made her lightheaded. She watched for a moment, transfixed by the sight. But then confusion clouded her exhausted brain. Did he not want her? Why was he in here taking care of his own needs without her? Insecurity crept in and she started to back out of the bathroom, ready to pretend she'd never seen it, when his eyes opened and their gazes tangled. His eyes glowed amber, his dark lashes rimming the gold and making them pop. She saw anguish in his face.

She took a breath and stepped forward. "May I join you?"

"GET OUT," he gritted through clenched teeth.

She flinched, but didn't move. "I'd like to help you with that," she said, her eyes flicking to his aching cock. Her nipples stood out in pebbled tips, her naked form almost too beautiful to take in.

He bit back the groan of longing that rose in his throat. His vision was razor-sharp, teeth elongating. He took several breaths to get control. "Get out," he croaked. "You're playing with fire."

"Maybe I like fire," she said softly, taking another step forward.

"Ashley," he bit out, "you don't know what I would do to you."

"What would you do?" Her gaze was soft, swimming in desire. Soft waves of rich brown hair fell in around her flushed face, and the blue eyes were almost all pupil. Jesus, that look... his flesh prickled with needles and pins, the need to mark her overtaking him. He imagined claiming her, taking her roughly from behind as he sank his teeth into her...

He gripped his cock, squeezing it hard as he pumped his fist up and down. Jesus Christ. He'd never been so out of control before. His climax came like a torpedo, shuddering through him. He shot his load onto the tile, his cum hot where it splattered on his hand and thigh.

Ashley stared, her blue eyes huge. She dragged her tongue across her lower lip, sending him into a second blinding orgasm. When it passed, he leaned against the shower wall, his knees weak. "Get out!" he barked.

She froze, looking uncertain.

"Go," he said, panting to regain his breath.

Her face flushed and he knew he'd hurt her, but he couldn't help it. She had no idea what would happen if he let his animal self loose with her. She'd be marked within seconds, possibly bleed to death, and if she survived, she'd be mated to a loser wolf with a death threat hanging over his head. Which meant she'd never be safe again.

"I'm sorry," she mumbled as she turned and slipped out the door without looking back.

He closed his eyes in frustration. He was such a jackass. He punched the shower wall beside him, cracking the tile. The pain eased a little of the need pulsing through him. The orgasm had only brought him the mildest relief. The pressure to claim the intoxicating female in the next room still pulsed beneath the surface. It was going to be a long night.

He turned off the water and toweled off, putting his boxers and jeans back on. He needed as much of a barrier between his cock and Ashley as possible. When he emerged, he found the lights off and Ashley curled up on the bed in fetal position. He could hear by her breath that she wasn't asleep, but her eyes were closed as if she were pretending to be. Guilt washed over him. How could he explain himself?

He couldn't.

He grabbed a pillow from the bed and settled in the armchair by the window. He'd sleep there, as far away from the beautiful human in his bed. No, it wasn't his bed. And she wasn't his female.

"You can share the bed with me," she said. She sounded hurt.

"No, I don't think I can," he said.

She sat up, peering through the darkness at him. He knew her human eyes couldn't make out much, but he saw every line of her pinched face. "Please?" she asked in a small voice.

If his insides were a dishtowel, she'd just twisted them and wrung him out. How could he deny her anything? He unfolded his long frame from the chair and crawled over the bed.

Rolling her to face away from him, he settled at her back, draping an arm around her waist. "I'm right here," he murmured in her ear.

She gave a contented sigh and laced her fingers through his, pulling his hand to her chest. He willed his brain not to think about the heat of her body or the rightness of the way she fit against him. Surprisingly, despite her proximity, he did relax and sleep overcame him long before he expected it.

7

—————

He dreamed Ashley was leaning over him, murmuring something seductive in his ear. She unbuttoned his jeans, her hand sliding into the opening and gripping his shaft.

He groaned out loud and the sound of his voice jerked him awake. He blinked, still in a haze from the dream. Light filtered through the motel room curtains.

His cock was hard and… oh, God.

Ashley had it in her grip, stroking his length.

He lay on his side and she pressed against his back, her soft form molded against his hard one. He groaned again. "What are you doing?" he croaked.

"We humans call it a hand job," she teased, the lilt of her voice like an intoxicating spell whispered in his ear. "But I'm willing to up the ante." She crawled over him, pulling off his jeans.

He found himself powerless to shake her off, or even to ask her to stop. It was so wrong, but he wanted it, wanted anything she was willing to give to him.

She returned to his cock, gripping it in one hand as she lowered her lips. He shuddered before she even met his flesh, his skin anticipating her wet heat. He reached up and held the headboard to keep from touching her, closed his eyes to keep from seeing her. His hips jolted off the bed the moment she made contact with her mouth.

"Oh, fuuu—" He cut off the curse, not wanting to be crude. She deserved better than that. She deserved a much better male than he.

Her lips closed around the head of his cock, tongue swirling around the rim.

His toes flexed involuntarily, legs stretched, buttocks clenched as his manhood stood even taller, growing for her.

She gripped him with two hands, sliding them up and down as she brought the head of his cock in and out of her mouth, making it feel like she'd taken his entire length into her mouth.

Her teeth grazed him more than once, her jaw too small for his width, but he didn't care. He wanted it to go on forever. He wanted it to stop immediately. He needed to claim her. *No.* He shook his head, shoving back the beast.

Ashley continued her meticulous torture,

humming against his skin, licking, sucking. His knuckles turned white on the headboard, muscles straining.

Cum surged down his shaft. "Oh, God," he choked. "I'm coming."

Ashley didn't take her mouth off his cock, accepting his offering with feminine grace, swallowing with a satisfied smile.

He flipped her to her back and pounced, covering her body with his. His cock, still hard despite the release, found her slick entryway and was already prodding for entrance before his brain kicked back into gear.

Get off her.

He blinked, rocking his hips so the tip of his cock actually breached her hole. Oh, hallelujah. Nothing felt sweeter than the first parting of her inner lips.

No.

He mustered all his willpower and yanked himself off her. *Get a grip, Stone.* Crawling down, he yanked her panties to the side and licked into her. She parted her thighs, drawing her knees up to make room for him. Her hips arched, her flat belly quivering at the flick of his tongue. She had a neatly trimmed pussy: petite and beautiful.

He stopped, his thoughts suddenly running in a direction that turned him cold.

"Who do you keep this pussy trimmed for?" he demanded, not managing to sound casual.

"You," she said thickly, wiggling her hips for more.

He frowned. "No, really. Who?"

She leaned up on her forearms, her brow furrowed at the interruption, or maybe because he had no right to ask. "For myself. I like it that way, okay?"

He relaxed and touched the pad of his thumb to her clit, gently vibrating.

She bucked, moaning something incomprehensible.

He pinned her hips down, parted her inner lips, and traced her dewy opening. She gave a closed-mouthed scream when he slid inside her—a needy cry that made his cock furious to be so far from her.

Using the palm of his hand to rub her sensitive nub, he slid in and out with his thumb, still holding her down as she thrashed beneath his ministrations. He changed fingers, sliding two inside and flicking his tongue over her clit.

She tugged on his hair, clamped her knees around his ears, and made a throaty cry.

Her responsiveness nearly sent him over the edge—she looked so beautiful with her hair fanned out on the pillow, her lithe body undulating and arching into his hands. He swirled a slow circle around her clit with his tongue, then sucked it. He fit three fingers inside her soaking pussy, then made a cone of his fingers and thumb and pumped it in and out, stretching her wide to accept him. She went wild, her eyes rolling back, fingernails sinking into his shoulders as she came, rubbing her clit over his face. He continued penetrating her tight cunt until the fluttering of her muscles around his fingers had stopped and she collapsed back on the bed.

He must have already been partially shifting, ready to mark her, because he realized his vision had changed. He scrambled backward off the bed, back to the shower where he blasted the cold water. Shucking his clothes, he climbed in and put his face and cock in the freezing stream.

Damn. The blowjob hadn't lessened his blue balls even by a measure. Water streamed over his heated body, cooling his skin but not the inner burn. His cock barely deflated. He jerked the shower curtain open when he finished and stalked past Ashley, who was coming into the bathroom, blushing.

He was an asshole. He didn't even know how to be nice to a woman, especially not one he wanted to fuck six ways to Friday or Sunday, or whatever the saying was. He heard the shower start up and ignored his cock's eager idea to rush back and join her.

The sound of her phone ringing jerked him out of his lustful haze. He dived for her purse and pulled it out, then jogged to the bathroom. Turning off the water in the shower, he thrust the phone at her.

She grabbed it, her eyes wide and frightened. "H-hello?"

He heard the electronic voice clearly, his hearing far more sensitive than a human's. "Midnight, downtown Greyhound bus terminal parking lot."

"Oka—"

The line went dead before she'd spoken. He didn't know how it worked for Zolla, but if he needed a certain length of time for the call to go on, they'd failed.

Ashley's dripping hand shook as she handed him the phone back, her face pale.

He wanted to tell her everything would be all right, but he wasn't sure he believed it, and he'd never been one to lie. He just gave her a curt nod and closed the shower curtain.

ASHLEY PICKED AT HER FOOD. Even the toast seemed too heavy for her nervous belly. Ben's friend Zolla hadn't been able to pinpoint the location of the call, so they were no closer to getting Melissa than the night before. Ben sat in silence, his plate already clean, watching her with his brooding gaze. If she didn't know better, she'd think he was angry with her, but by now, she was used to his scowls and dark looks. Whatever it was that went on in that brain of his, whatever his mysterious thoughts, she was fairly certain he liked her. Which didn't mean she felt any safer or more confident with him.

She didn't know why he hadn't had sex with her, or why he seemed almost disgruntled about the blowjob she'd given him, but she had noticed that despite his orgasm, his flag had still been flying at full mast. Maybe sex was different for shifters.

"Do you think she's okay?" she asked.

He pursed his lips. "I don't know what to think. I know it's a good thing they still seem to want my laptop. I guess we'd better figure out why."

He lifted his palm in greeting and she twisted to see his friend Zolla walking through the diner toward them. She slid over to make room for him in their booth and Ben immediately shook his head.

Zolla seemed to understand. He held out his palm in a gentlemanly gesture. "I'm sure you prefer to sit with Ben," he said.

Her gaze flicked from one wolf to the other, and then she shrugged and scooted out of her side, sliding in next to Ben.

"So you were saying we need to figure out why they want your laptop," Zolla said.

"How could you possibly have heard that from

way across the diner?" she asked, thinking he must read lips or something.

Zolla smirked. "Wolf ears. All the better to hear you with."

She laughed and Ben looked at her askance, as if she shouldn't be laughing at another man's jokes.

A waitress came by and Zolla ordered a coffee.

"So what's on the laptop?"

Ben shrugged. "It's my access point to everything, but I don't store anything of importance on it. I'm thinking they could be after all my passwords? Could a hacker get that info from my computer?"

Zolla nodded. "Yes. I set up the initial security for your brother's system. I made it so it was un-hackable from the outside. If things are still the same, then yes, your laptop and only your laptop would provide them what they need to get in." He looked grim. "Not even Jack had universal access, although he asked me for it more than once."

"He asked me for it, too," Ben muttered.

Zolla gave him a sharp look and Ben cocked his head by a fraction of an inch. "It's possible," Ben said.

"That Jack is behind this?" she asked, trying to understand the unspoken conversation.

Ben gave a single nod.

"What did you find out from the license plate?"

"Registered to a Dan Walker. Typical thug—

several misdemeanors, one felony for car theft. Probably not the mastermind behind this, but a hired goon." Zolla slid a piece of paper across the table. "Here's his address, although I doubt you'll find him there."

"And no info on this morning's call?" Ashley asked, although she already knew the answer.

He shook his head. "Location information has been removed from your sister's phone and the call was too short to do a traditional trace," he said, looking sympathetic. "I'm sorry."

"Thanks. I really appreciate your help."

Ben seemed to bristle next to her, as if he didn't like her talking to him.

Zolla looked away from her and asked, "Have you talked to Stanley?"

Ben's jaw clenched. "Yeah. He was pretty butt-hurt about me calling in a favor when I wasn't technically a member of their pack. I don't think I can count on their help for the meetup."

Zolla said nothing for a long moment, just tapped the fork against the spoon. Then he blew out his breath. "You know he wants you to lead the pack, right?"

A muscle jumped in Ben's face. "Not going to happen."

Zolla shrugged. "Well, Stanley's losing wolves right and left. He lost me. He's not strong enough to lead. No one wants to follow a beta. I know that must sound ripe coming from me."

Ben didn't answer.

"Well, I have a contract job in Edgewater, so I'll be out all day, unless you want me to stick around."

Ben shook his head.

"Do you two want to hang at my place today?"

"Maybe," Ben said. "It would be about an unlikely a place to stay, one where no one would think to look."

"Well, if you decide you want to, here's the address and the code to get in."

"Thanks. I think we will go there."

"Okay, then I'll meet you there an hour before the meeting."

"Good. I'll see if Mark Ruhl will come as well. Thank you."

BEN OPENED the car door for her, but instead of stepping in, she turned to face him. "What's with the weird vibe if I even look at Zolla?" she demanded.

He avoided her eyes, looking over the top of the car toward the Flatiron Mountains, which jutted majestically in the background. His body itched to shift and run for that wilderness, to get rid of all this pent-up tension winding his crank.

"You're acting crazy," she said.

He knew she was right. His behavior was over the top, even by wolf standards. He dragged his eyes to meet her. "I know," he admitted. "I'm sorry. I just can't seem to help myself around you."

"Well, you can relax, because I'm only interested in you," she said, laying a palm on his chest.

Her touch burned him like a branding iron, causing him to jerk at the jolt of electricity that passed between them. But as much as he adored her, as much as he wanted her, he couldn't have her. And pretending otherwise, when she was making her feelings plain, would be cruel.

"Ashley… I can't." He looked around as if the right words would be posted on a sign nearby. "I can't do this with you."

She stiffened. "Why not?" she asked, her voice sounding tight.

He ran his fingers through his hair. "I just can't. I'm sorry. It's not possible. I shouldn't have," he swallowed, "done what I did last night—or this morning. I know I'm an asshole. You don't deserve this."

Her face turned to stone and she shrugged like it didn't matter, climbing in the car. He hesitated, his hand on the door handle. But what else was there to say? Explaining the marking thing would only terrify her. Besides, even if marking wasn't an issue, he couldn't get involved with her. He couldn't let another person he cared about die on his watch. He shut her door and walked around to the driver's side.

They rode in silence for twenty minutes before she said, "Is there another woman?"

"No," he snapped, not meaning to sound so harsh.

She flinched and turned to look out her window.

He waited for the next question, but it never came. They made it all the way to Zolla's without speaking another word. He pulled into the driveway and used the code he'd given him to open the garage door. When he returned to the car to pull it in, Ashley had climbed over to the driver's seat.

"I'll see you later," she muttered, trying to shut the door he'd left agape.

He shoved his hand in between, and managed to slow it a bit before it slammed on him.

Ashley's face registered horror and she shoved the door back open to free him. He used the opportunity to put his entire body between the door and the car, reaching in to haul her out.

"Stop it," she cried, struggling.

Afraid of leaving finger bruises on her arms, he spun her around and wrapped one arm around her waist to pick her up. "Where did you think you were going?"

"I don't know—away from here! What do you care? I'll be at the meetup."

His need to protect her made his teeth sharpen in his mouth and a growl to erupt from his throat.

She froze, her shoulders hunching in a slight cower, but her voice came out strong and brave. "So I'm still your prisoner, huh?"

"Yeah," he muttered. "You're still my prisoner." He pushed her over the hood of the car and began to rain smacks down on her wriggling ass, hard and fast.

"Ben!" she shrieked, the panic of public humiliation evident in the pitch of her voice.

"Don't even think about going anywhere without me," he growled. He continued spanking, not because he thought she deserved punishment, but just to assert his dominance. He didn't expect to earn her submission, though. Hell, he was probably forever sealing the end of their relationship, which should be what he wanted. Except… there was no way he could let her go.

"Okay, stop!" she yelled, turning to look over her shoulder at him. Her face held a mixture of emotions—her eyes dark and glassy, her teeth bared, her brows down low in anger.

"You can't leave," he growled. "It's not safe."

She didn't answer, so he delivered several more hard slaps.

"Ashley? Do you understand?"

"Yes, *sir*," she said, sarcasm dripping from her voice.

He turned her around and placed his shoulder into the fold of her hips to toss her over his back, inadvertently lifting her skirt up. When he reached to pull it down, he brushed across her panties and found them soaked. Even when she was pissed at him, her body said yes. His cock went rock hard. How could he doubt she was his mate? Their chemistry was off the charts.

She smacked his back with her palm. "Put me down, you big jerk. I've had enough of your Neanderthal ways. I've had enough of you."

"I'm sure you have," he said, carrying her into the garage and opening the door to the house. "Unfortunately, you have no choice but to put up with me for one more day." He plopped her on the sofa. "Do I need to find the duct tape?"

She surged to her feet, a wild look of defiance on her face. "Yes!"

He hid a surprised smile. *Yes?* What did that mean? Wicked thoughts crept into his brain. "Okay," he said and tugged her back up to stand. Whirling her around, he pinned her wrists behind her back. He used them to force her to the end of the sofa, where he pushed her down over the padded arm.

"You need to be restrained, Ashley?" he asked, his voice low and gravelly.

Her breathing came in audible gasps.

He leaned his body over hers, his erection pressing into her soft ass. "Do you like being my prisoner?" he murmured in her ear.

She didn't answer, but her hips pushed backward, the heat of her flesh searing against his straining cock. With a great effort of will, he wrenched his hips safely away from hers. He could not claim her. He shouldn't be doing this—not after he'd just told her they couldn't have a relationship. But the intoxicating scent of her wet pussy had sent reason flying.

Keeping her wrists pinned with one hand, he used the other to lift her skirt and tug down her panties. Her cheeks were reddened from the spanking he'd just given her, and she clenched them now, as if to ward off further spanks.

He tested to be sure he was reading her correctly. "Spread your legs, Ashley."

Her feet slid apart.

His cock surged against his zipper, painfully hard.

He brought his hand up between her legs, slapping her pussy.

She shrieked, trying to lift her torso, but he didn't allow it. He noted she did not close her legs.

He slapped her again, her natural lubricant coating his fingers. He spanked her little pussy over and over again until she began to whimper and plead. "Please… Ben… please."

"Please what?"

"I—please… fuck me."

He was unprepared for his body's reaction to that request. His skin flushed and prickled, canines lengthened, vision changed.

Do. Not. Mark her.

He forced himself to inhale several times through his nose, the effort to stay in control overwhelming. When his vision dulled again, he nudged her feet even wider. Using the pad of his middle finger, he stroked along her dewy slit, gliding between her inner lips, gathering moisture, and dragging it up to her clit.

She gave a wavering moan.

He flicked her responsive little button and her knees buckled, her feet sliding out from under her. The sofa bore her weight and he pressed her pinned wrists down, holding her in place as he continued to torture her most sensitive organ.

Her moans grew louder, a needy, desperate pitch taking over.

He slid two fingers inside her.

She mewled, arching against the hold he had on her wrists.

He pumped his fingers in and out. It only took a few strokes before she cried out, her muscles gripping his fingers, squeezing in a rhythmic pulse.

"Ben," she choked and the sound of his name on her lips nearly turned him savage.

Somehow, he managed to ease his fingers out without pouncing on her and making her forever his. He slapped her pussy one more time as he backed away. The change was still upon him—his entire body shook with the effort to keep it back. He needed to shift and run—to get release this pent-up frustration.

"Promise me you'll stay put," he said, his voice still rough.

She said nothing.

He slapped her bare ass and she yelped. "I promise!"

He released her wrists and pulled her panties up, then turned her to face him and pinched her nipple between his thumb and forefinger, twisting as her eyes widened. "You're killing me," he muttered, even though he knew he was the one doing the killing. He'd been the king of mixed signals, dragging her, and her heart—if she cared for him, and he desperately hoped she did—through the wringer.

AFTER PINCHING HER NIPPLE, Ben walked toward the bedroom, yanking off his t-shirt. He was the picture of masculine power, his lean muscles of his naked torso rippling with movement. She'd seen the bulge of his erection, and yet, once again, he hadn't claimed her. Despite her orgasm moments ago, her body thought only of being under him, his huge cock penetrating her, making her scream as he took her roughly.

She hardly knew what to think about where they stood. After licking her wounds in the car, she knew she had no reason to be upset. He'd never made her any promises. She was disappointed and hurt, and didn't like feeling like she'd been dumped, but she was still certain that Ben Stone felt something for her. Maybe it was just physical attraction, maybe it was something more.

All she knew was he made her feel desirable and sexy. He made her feel other things she'd never felt before. Crazy things—like she would willingly let him string her wrists from the ceiling and whip her with his belt again if that turned him on. Because in retrospect, it sure as hell turned her on. She squeezed her bottom, feeling the sting that still lingered from his spanking. She adored his dominance, found his power intoxicating. The thought of him punishing her again made her cream her panties. She didn't understand it, but she definitely wanted more.

She should have pressed him more about why he couldn't be with her. She'd been afraid of what answer he might give and had chosen to take personal offense rather than keep a cool head and just try to understand him. Now her mind had conjured a million possibilities. Maybe humans and shifters literally couldn't mate. Or maybe it was against their rules to be with a human.

Except Zolla had said something about Ben marking her, which implied that they could take human lovers. What did marking her mean?

She heard the bedroom door bump and the largest black wolf she'd ever seen came trotting out. She drew a breath and held it, her skin prickling. Even knowing it was Ben, she still found the beast terrifying. He stood higher than her waist, with thick black fur and huge jowls. He trotted toward the rear of the house, where a doggy door had been installed. Before he left, he turned to look at her, as if in warning.

"I know, I know. I'm staying right here."

The wolf's jaws opened, revealing a row of vicious teeth, but she could have sworn he was smiling at her. It reminded her of her first day working for him and she smiled back, despite her pride. The wolf lowered himself to squeeze through the door, which was too small for him, and ran out.

She curled up the sofa and buried herself in the book she'd found on Zolla's shelf. At first she didn't think she'd be able to concentrate, but her mind was so thrilled with a distraction—any distraction from her worry over Melissa and her situation with

Ben—that she found herself swept away to an alien planet.

She didn't re-emerge for a couple hours, when her stomach started growling. She padded to the front door and opened it, looking around for Ben. The wolf was sitting on the front steps. He turned and bared his teeth at her.

She froze, her body having an autonomic reaction to the danger an enormous, snarling wolf presented. Reason took over, and she forced herself to step out and sit down on the step beside him.

Ben got up, shoving his nose under her thigh, as if to make her stand, too. When she didn't, she saw teeth again. He bit the fabric of her skirt and tugged, making a growling sound. Refusing to be cowed by him, as terrifying as he may be, she rubbed his head. "Okay, okay, I'll go back in. But I'm hungry. Aren't you?"

He leaned his body against her legs, pressing her forward and through the door.

She laughed. "All right, I'm in. You want me to see if there's any food here?"

The wolf looked toward the kitchen.

"Okay. Let's see what your friend Zolla keeps in his cupboards."

She walked to the kitchen and opened the fridge, which only contained a few take-out containers, beer, and condiments. She opened the cabinets. He had plenty of non-perishables: cans of soup, beans, macaroni and cheese packages. She pulled out a couple of cans of chili. "You probably want meat, right?"

She searched the drawer for a can opener and, finding one, opened the can.

She wondered if Ben would shift back. In a way, it was easier with him in wolf form. She wouldn't be offended by his lack of conversation. And it was hard to be mad at a wolf.

She dumped the chili into two bowls and heated it up in the microwave. "I'm actually a good cook, not that you'll be able to tell from this meal. Maybe someday you'll let me cook for you. What was up with neither you nor Karen eating my banana bread? That was downright rude."

The wolf's mouth opened again and she thought he was laughing at her.

"What? It was. What's up with you and Karen, anyway?"

When the wolf actually rolled his eyes, she chuckled. "No? Nothing?"

He stepped around her and she instinctively backed away, then gave a nervous laugh. The kitchen seemed tiny with his huge four-legged body taking up space. "It's hard not to be intimidated by you," she said. Forcing herself to conquer her fear, she stepped forward and held out her hand for him to sniff.

She thought he might be laughing at her again.

She buried both hands in his fur, rubbing his soft ears and the thick fur at the scruff of his neck. "You sure are beautiful."

He held still for it, but she couldn't tell whether he liked it or not. Maybe being pet like a dog was beneath a werewolf.

The microwave beeped and she took their bowls out, setting his on the floor at his feet. "Sorry if that's not how you eat. I'm new at this."

It seemed fine, because he cleaned his bowl in about one minute flat. She'd only taken a few bites in the time it took him to eat. "Do you want more?"

He gave a little chuff, which she took to be affirmative, so she opened another can of chili and heated it up for him. She stared at his huge form as he ate. He was as tall as a Great Dane—the kind of dog you make jokes about riding like a horse.

If they had children together, they could ride him. Sheesh, where did that thought come from? They weren't having children together. They weren't even dating. They got each other off and that was the end of it.

THOUGH HE HATED BEING INDOORS when in wolf form, he hung around with Ashley that afternoon.

He had run to Ashley's place when he first went out and sniffed around. People had definitely been there. He made a note of the scents. Even if they managed to get her sister back, he didn't think Ashley would be safe. Not until they figured out who was behind all this. But where could she and her sister go? And who would watch over them? It could take weeks or even months for this plot to unravel.

He actually thought Zolla's place was as safe as any, and he did trust the wolf.

Ashley read for a while, but as dusk came on, she grew restless, pacing about the room.

"Do you think they ever had any intention of returning Melissa?" she asked him.

He figured it was rhetorical, since he couldn't speak. He preferred it that way, anyway.

She looked at him, a pinched look tightening her face. "I kind of don't. They weren't wearing any masks or anything. Which means, either they're really stupid and they don't care if we can identify them, or they planned to kill us both."

He had arrived at the same conclusion, which was why he wasn't letting Ashley out of his sight.

She paced some more. "I probably should've just called the police when I got the first message."

He glared at her.

"No?" Her shoulders sagged. "I guess not. You can't really have police poking in your business, but I'm starting to think… Well, we're sort of outnumbered. Even if you are a wolf who doesn't mind bullet holes. I mean, Melissa and I aren't bullet-proof." A darker shadow crossed her face. "If Melissa's still alive."

He trotted over and put his muzzle against her leg in a show of protection and comfort.

She rubbed his head. Sinking down on the sofa, she took his face between her hands, rubbing his ears. "I'm scared, Ben," she whispered, unshed tears glimmering in her eyes.

He licked her hand. To hell with this. He wasn't going to let her grow more and more frightened as they holed up here for another six hours. He trotted toward the bedroom, shifting as he walked. When he turned to shut the door, he saw Ashley craning her neck to watch him, getting an eyeful of his naked form, and damn if he didn't still have a raging erection for her. Her mouth opened when their eyes caught, and he gave her a half-grin, watching as her eyes widened and a blush spread across her cheeks.

He shut the door and changed into his clothes. "Come on," he said, walking briskly out and taking her hand to tug her off the sofa.

"Where are we going?"

"Out," he said, tugging her toward the garage. "You're sick of being cooped up here, and so am I."

He opened her door for her. She gazed up in bewilderment.

"There's a taco place down the street that smells

good. Can you walk in those shoes?" He wished he had somehow arranged to get her a change of clothes today. The poor girl was still in her work skirt and heels and the mauve t-shirt from Shayla.

She tugged her skirt down, as if it might cover more of her long, bare legs. "Yeah, definitely. How far?"

"Only a block. I'll carry you if you get tired."

She licked her lips, making his cock jerk in his pants. Flushing, she looked away. "That won't be necessary," she said, her voice huskier than usual.

Abruptly, he found himself pushing her up against the house, his body pressing against her soft curves. He cupped the side of her face, lifting it as if he was going to kiss her. He stopped himself just in time, freezing as he realized the inappropriateness of his actions. He'd just told her he couldn't be in a relationship with her. What the hell was he doing?

He brushed his lips across her forehead, then her temple, then her lush lips. "Ashley... I'm a whole bundle of trouble. Look where working for me has already landed you—" He stopped, wanting to backpedal. He didn't want her to stop working for him, no matter what happened. The thought of going back to Stone Technologies without her made him feel dead. "What I'm trying to say is..." Well, what the hell was he trying to say? Being so close to her, feeling her body against his, having her scent in his nostrils made it hard to formulate any thought.

He stroked her cheek with his thumb, a sense of both longing and loss giving him a tenderness he didn't usually find. "Ashley, it's so complicated. And I'm just... sorry."

She thrust her chin forward in a cute show of defiance. "What is it? Why can't you be with me? Just tell me."

"It's too dangerous. You're human and I'm... not."

She blinked rapidly, pushing him away from her and averting her face.

"I'm sorry," he repeated, standing back and extending his arm to allow her to pass him.

THEY WALKED down the street together, side by side. She felt dizzy from having his hard body pressed against hers, the aggressive way he pinned her sending a heady rush of lust rocketing through her body. Her emotions warred between anger and acceptance. She did believe Ben was sorry, but she didn't want his apology, she wanted him.

"Ben?"

As usual for him, he didn't answer, but he did look over.

"Do you miss Venezuela?" she asked.

It was the wrong thing to say. His mask slid back in place, lines hardening. "No," he said, but it seemed like a lie—she saw pain in his expression. She remembered, belatedly, that his brother and father had been killed there. If she'd heard right, it had been some kind of grotesque death—like a wild animal... Oh. A wolf, of course.

"What happened there?" she asked softly. She held her breath, not really expecting an answer.

To her surprise, he spoke. "My father's pack had been threatened takeover by another—a drug cartel of shifters. My brother had flown in to help him fight, but..." He swallowed and didn't go on.

"I'm sorry," she said. "And your mother? Is she still alive?"

He shook his head. "No. She died when I was twelve of cancer. Which isn't supposed to affect wolves," he said bitterly.

For once, she had nothing to say. She knew he didn't want her pity. She reached out and touched his hand. He instantly laced his fingers through hers.

"I think—" he said, then cleared his throat. "I think she just didn't want to go on living with my dad. He was a top-notch asshole, like me."

Her chest tightened and her nose tickled, tears rising up for him. "That's not you. You may play that part, but I know it's not the real you."

He lifted his eyes, looking stunned. She met his gaze evenly, transmitting her utter confidence in her statement. As if he couldn't take it, he literally shook it off, like a dog shakes off water.

"I mean it. Sure, you're a dick at times—okay, most of the time, but underneath it all, you are sweet."

"No," he said. "I'm really not. And you're the only person on the planet who has ever described me that way."

"Because I know the truth," she said, lifting her chin and daring him to contradict her.

His expression wavered for a moment and he looked uncertain or lost. Then he did the same shaking motion he'd done a few minutes before. "No, you don't," he said bitterly.

"What would it take for you to accept anything I offer? Do you always have to reject it?" She almost said *reject me,* because that was the truth of the matter.

He didn't answer. They had reached the taco place, and he led her inside, glancing at the board. "Do you know what you want?"

It was an authentic Mexican joint, with the menu mostly in Spanish. She shrugged. "Surprise me."

Ben ordered in Spanish and they handed him a couple of Dos Equis beers with lime wedges stuffed in the mouth. He passed one to her and they sat down at a booth.

"What did you order?"

"A *carne asada* burrito. Is that okay?"

"Yeah," she said with a little laugh.

"You don't know what that is, do you?"

She grinned sheepishly. "Some kind of burrito."

"It's a marinated beefsteak. I think you'll like it."

It was stupid, but she leaned forward and said, "Speak to me in Spanish?"

His eyebrows shot up.

She shrugged. "I like the way it sounds."

"*Como qué?*"

"Keep going."

"*Si pudiera decirte la verdad, deciré que tu eres… mi todo mundo.*"

His words rolled over her ears like they were spoken by Don Juan himself. "What did you say?"

He hesitated long enough for her to realize that he'd said something real for once. Something he couldn't or wouldn't say in English. She tried to replay the syllables in her mind to decipher their meaning, but her high school Spanish was lacking. Was it something about speaking the truth and then, *you are my whole world?* She clung to that thought, and placed it in her heart like a little jewel to take out and hold to the light the next time he rejected her.

8

They met Mark and Zolla back at Zolla's house. Ashley headed toward the bathroom to change her clothes. He watched the shape of her ass under the red skirt as she sashayed away. God, how he ached to be inside her, to spank those lovely cheeks and fuck her from behind. Or maybe, even, to take her ass.

"You should really mark her," Zolla said.

He frowned. "What's it to you?"

To the omega's credit, he didn't cower under Ben's narrowed gaze. "It would calm you down. You'd be able to think straight when she's around."

His lip curled in disbelief. He'd never heard that about mating a female. Besides, it was an impossibility. "She's human."

"So, it just means you have to be careful. Go for the shoulder instead of the neck. Avoid major arteries. She'll heal up all right. She looks healthy enough."

His vision changed and a growl erupted from his throat. He didn't like Zolla talking about the way she looked. He didn't like him talking about her at all.

Zolla held up his hands and lifted his chin, baring his throat to show subservience. "Hey, this is what I'm talking about. Once she's marked you won't be so crazy to let us all know she's yours."

"Fuck you," he muttered. Turning to Mark, he said, "Did you bring the vest for her?"

"Yes," Mark said, unzipping a duffel bag. "I have several Kevlar vests here, as well as firearms, in case you want to stay in human form."

"I don't. It's just Ashley I'm worried about." He found he couldn't drop the topic of marking Ashley, though. Turning back to Zolla, he said, "If you were me—a wolf with more than one enemy who wants him dead—would you mark a female?"

Zolla tipped his head to the side. "Maybe not, but you might be able to think your way out of this better if you weren't so jacked up on her pheromones."

Ashley returned, her slight figure making her seem so vulnerable, so human. His blood surged to protect her. But in this case, protecting her would be keeping her away from him.

He held a vest open for her. "I need you to wear this for the meeting," he told her.

"Bulletproof?" she asked, looking from him to Mark.

"Yes, ma'am," Mark answered. "But your head is still vulnerable, so keep it down if any shots are fired."

"Here's how it's going to go," Ben cut in. "You're going to drive up there, and make the trade. Obviously I interrupted it too early last time, and I'm sorry for that," he said.

Ashley's eyebrows raised in surprise. He knew it was out of character for him to apologize for anything.

"As soon as your sister is released, the two of you are going to get in your car and drive straight back here. Keep an eye on the rearview mirrors to make sure you're not followed."

"What will you do?"

"We're going to attack," he said, looking at the two men to make sure they were on board. They both nodded their assent.

"If anything goes awry and we're forced to come out before the trade is made—and I hope it won't—" he added at her look of alarm, "then you get in your car and drive off. I will make sure we get your sister back and I will tear out the throats of every last one of her captors."

She swallowed.

"Do you understand?"

"Yes, sir," she said.

"What happens if fighting breaks out?" he quizzed her.

"I get in the car and drive back here."

"Good girl."

THEY DROVE DOWNTOWN. He rode with Ashley, instructing her to let him out a few blocks before the bus station. "Remember the plan?" he asked.

Her face was pale and drawn, but she nodded without hesitation.

"What do you do?"

"I get Melissa and drive away as fast as I can."

"And if something goes wrong?"

"I get in the car and drive away."

"No matter what. Don't stay to watch." He wrote a phone number down on a piece of paper and handed it to her. "If something really goes wrong, and we never come back to the apartment, call Shayla. Tell her what happened and she'll help you. Got it?"

Ashley's eyes had grown very round and her lips were trembling.

He cupped her face with both his hands, his thumb stroking her lips. "No, no. Shh. Nothing like that will happen. I'm just providing insurance, that's all. I'm going to take care of this."

"Okay," she said, her voice cracking.

"That's my brave girl." He leaned forward, meaning to kiss her forehead, but his instinct to claim her took over. He took her mouth in a bruising kiss, sweeping his tongue against the seam of her lips until she yielded entry. He slid his hand from her face to her nape, holding her prisoner as he kissed and sucked at her lips as if they were his only salvation. It felt as if they were. When they finally broke apart, breathless, she stared up at him with a dazed look. He gave her one last kiss, then another before he forced himself to turn away.

"I'm going to leave my clothes in the car," he said, opening the door and standing up to shuck his clothing. He dropped them in the seat, shut the door, and shifted, ignoring the screaming in his brain that said not to let her go into danger.

Cold sweat dampened her shirt under the bulletproof vest as she pulled the car into the Greyhound parking lot. Her entire body trembled and her hands were ice cold on the wheel. She parked in a space and grabbed the laptop, stepping out. She looked around. The lot was full of cars, but she saw no sign of movement, nor did she hear any voices.

She turned back to her car and put the keys loosely back in the ignition so it would be ready to drive off at a moment's notice, if necessary. She left the door slightly ajar, as well. Then she walked out toward the middle of the lot.

Time ticked by, glacially slow. Where were the wolves? She peered in the shadows, looking low for the glowing eyes, but saw nothing. Still, she sensed Ben was there, somewhere. She paced up and down the lot, but no one appeared.

Maybe she should wait in the car.

She turned and started back.

A car pulled into the lot, its headlights blinding her. She covered her eyes and watched as it drove past her, up to the main building. A woman got out of the passenger side and ran up the steps, trying to open the locked door to the station. She turned and trotted back down the stairs and got in the car, saying something to the driver. The car turned around and drove out.

She exhaled. Not them. Well, where in the hell were they? She pulled out her phone and glanced at the time. Twelve fifteen. It felt like an hour had already passed. She forced herself to take a deep breath to the count of four, then held it until she thought her lungs would explode. When she blew it out, her body relaxed marginally. She tried a second time.

Three pairs of headlights swung in at once.

Nice cars—not like last time in the Stone parking lot. Two black 4Runners and a dark blue Mercedes. Not cars that belonged in a Greyhound bus station. Her heart jumped erratically in her chest. She turned in a circle, then forced herself to just stand still and wait.

They stopped in a ring around her. Her eyes slid toward her vehicle at least one hundred feet away now. Damn. She should've just waited in her car. Why was she so stupid?

She peered at the cars, trying to see if her sister might be in one, but with the headlights shining in her eyes, she couldn't see anything.

The door of the four-runner in front of her swung open. "Put the laptop down and back away," he said.

"Where's Melissa?" she demanded, wishing her voice didn't sound so high-pitched and shaky.

She heard the sound of a gun cocking as the man extended his arm straight out, sighting her with a pistol in his hand. "Do it now."

"Where's Melissa?" she repeated. "I'm not giving you anything until I see my sister."

The man fired his gun and the bullet struck near her feet. A scream erupted from her throat and she jumped, almost dropping the laptop, her entire body shaking so hard she'd lost all coordination. She wondered if the sound of gunshots would bring the cops.

She caught a shadow moving between cars. Ben. It gave her courage. "Show me Melissa and I'll hand over the laptop."

The man starting walking toward her at a menacing stride. Several other figures emerged from the cars, all closing in. A snarl tore through the air and a man screamed as Ben took him down.

"There's her dog! Shoot it," the first man yelled, not moving his aim from her and continuing to walk purposely forward.

She backed away, but he was upon her. He fired his gun right at her chest, just above where she held the laptop. She flew back and landed on her back from the force of it, a searing pain over her heart causing her to lose her breath. The laptop flew from her hands and skidded across the asphalt.

"Hey, watch the laptop, you idiot," one of the men yelled at the shooter as he scooped it up.

She struggled to breathe, the wind knocked out of her. *Hit but not hurt.* She reminded herself she was wearing the vest and rolled to her side, wincing at the pain.

A light gray wolf arced over her body, flying at her attacker. He took the man down, tearing at his throat with a horrific snarl. It was a smaller wolf— not small, but normal wolf-sized. She caught the flash of a huge tan wolf launching through the air near the Mercedes and toppling a man despite the bullet he sank into him. Zolla and Mark.

She staggered to her feet, her breath still painful against her ribs. The gun had gone clattering to the asphalt and she snatched it up with her trembling fingers. Gripping the handle, she ducked her head and limped toward the four-runner, the laptop tucked under her arm.

She had to find Melissa.

She yanked open the back door as the sound of gunshots and growls still filled the air. The vehicle seemed empty. She stepped in to peer into the trunk. No one.

She climbed out. A high-pitched animal whine sent a shot of terror through her. Heart in her throat, she aimed the gun toward the sound. Ben was tussling with a man as several others fired shots into him. She pulled the trigger.

She missed, but the men turned and aimed their guns at her. She crouched down and ran for the next car. A driver still sat behind the wheel, which probably meant Melissa was in there. Staying bent in half, she raced around the car and popped up, pointing the muzzle of the gun through the open window, right at his temple.

"Where is she?"

Unnervingly, the man didn't look ruffled by the pistol she aimed at his head. "Not here," he said.

"Where?" she hissed through clenched teeth, tapping the gun against his head.

He shook his head. "She isn't here." He gave her a greasy smile. "Too bad for you."

She wanted to shoot him. She thought about pulling the trigger, but morality won out. She wasn't prepared to take a life, even if they had killed her sister.

She backed slowly away, keeping the gun aimed at his head. The air still rippled with the confusion of shouts and growls. She backed toward the third car, but the man she held the gun on pulled out a gun of his own and fired it at her, but thankfully missed.

A flash of black fur flew over her and Ben was upon the man in the vehicle, tearing him out of the window, but taking at least five shots in the belly in the process.

"No," she screamed, running toward them.

The gray wolf sideswiped her, shoving her in the direction of her car. When she started again toward Ben, he bared his teeth at her, blocking her way.

"Zolla?" she asked, frightened of him despite the fact that she knew he was a friend.

He lunged forward, butting her legs with his head, once more pushing her toward her car.

"I have to find Melissa," she said, and darted around him the other way, to the third car. She pulled open the door and looked inside. Empty.

Unless her sister was in the trunk, the man had told the truth—she wasn't here.

A low moan of despair rose in her throat as her legs carried her, running, toward her car. What had happened to Melissa? Was she lying dead some-where? Had they meant the same fate for her?

She leaped in her vehicle and started it up, backing up with a screech of tires. Sirens sounded in the distance and she gunned the engine, shooting out the parking lot before the cops showed up. As she tore away, her phone rang in her purse. Pulling it out with shaking hands, she glanced at the caller.

Melissa.

WHEN THE POLICE cars screeched around the corner and entered the parking lot, he and the other two wolves disappeared under the protection of the shadows. He hadn't recognized any of the men, so he was no closer to knowing who was behind this attack, nor had they rescued Melissa. And dammit if Ashley hadn't nearly gotten herself killed, several times over. He couldn't focus for most of the fight, because he'd been too worried about protecting her.

She had blatantly disobeyed his instructions. They would be discussing that before all this was through.

Zolla and Mark followed him, slinking through

the darkness until they reached Mark's car where they shifted. All three were covered in blood, both their own and the men's. He regretted their injuries, and making sure they were all right became his first priority, since they had acted under his command.

Zolla opened the door to his car and handed out clothes. Ben shook his head. "I'll run back. I need the fresh air. How are you two?"

Mark looked down at the bullet wounds leaking blood on his torso. "Fine," he said in a clipped tone.

"You?" Ben asked Zolla.

The smaller wolf was panting, weakened by his injuries. "Nothing serious," he said.

"Are you sure? Can you drive?"

"I'll drive," Mark said decisively, his status outweighing Zolla's. Turning to Ben, he asked, "Did you recognize anyone?"

Ben shook his head. "Not a one. Any sign of Ashley's twin?"

"There was no female but Ashley," Zolla said definitively. "I sniffed all three cars. They didn't bring her."

Ben swore softly.

"You think she's dead?" Mark asked.

He met Mark's eyes, his stomach knotting for Ashley. "Seems like it," he said heavily. How in the hell was he going to tell her that? Red-hot anger on her behalf flooded him. "I'm going to kill every last one of them," he growled.

The way the two men looked at him told him they had his back. He experienced a rush of gratitude for their help that nearly choked him. He wasn't used to relying on others, or caring for anyone but himself. Rather than a burden of responsibility, the honor of their allegiance struck him hard. He needed them and they gave themselves freely, trusted his lead.

He grasped each man by the nape, bowing his head. "Thank you, brothers," he said gruffly. Unable to say more, he released them and cleared his throat.

"Did they get the laptop?" Zolla asked.

"Yes," he said. "Can you protect the data? I should've brought a decoy instead."

"No, this will provide the information we'll need. I'll track who uses your passwords and find their location. If the girl is still alive, we can get her. And If it's Jack, you'll know it and can take appropriate measures," Zolla said.

"All right, let's get back so you can start tracking. I'll meet you at your place. Ashley should be there already." He shifted back to wolf form and started running, relishing the feel of the run, the air in his fur cooling the heat of his murderous instincts.

9

Ashley swung onto the corner of Platte and 15th, the address her sister gave her and pulled over, peering into the shadows. She saw movement and Melissa came bursting out from behind the building, trailed by a young man. She threw open the car door and rushed to meet her sister, the two of them falling into each other's arms.

"Oh, my God, Melissa. Thank God. Thank God you're all right. Oh, my God," she said, hot tears spilling down her cheeks as she rocked her sister, not willing to release her from the hug.

"Come on," Melissa said, "let's get out of here."

"Are you okay?" she asked, stepping back to look at her. Melissa looked pale and tired; a yellow bruise stood out on her cheekbone and her lip was cut and swollen.

"I'll be a lot better when we get to your place."

"Who's this?" she asked, turning her attention to the man.

Melissa grabbed her sleeve and urged her toward the car, obviously nervous. "Jeremy. He helped me escape. Come on, let's go."

They piled in the car and Ashley took off for Zolla's. "So tell me what happened."

Melissa drew a breath, then closed her eyes and leaned her head back. "I'll tell you everything, but can it wait? I just want to get somewhere I can breathe."

Ashley reached over and squeezed her sister's hand. "I can't believe you got away. I was so afraid I'd never see you again," she said, tears popping into her eyes again.

Melissa returned the squeeze, twisting to look over her shoulder, as if fearful they were being followed. Jeremy, who had climbed in the back seat, reached forward and put his hand on her sister's shoulder.

Ashley drove as fast as she could without attracting attention to Zolla's house, entering with the code to the garage door Ben had given her. "Come in, this place is safe. Ben should be back soon." She spoke with confidence, but a twinge of fear gripped her stomach as she remembered the sound of animals yelping every time a shot had been fired into one of the shifters. Were they invincible? Or could they be killed if they were shot enough or in the right places? No, she couldn't think that way. Ben would come.

She led them inside and showed Melissa to the bathroom where she could get cleaned up. She brought her sister some ice for her bruise. "This is for your face."

Her sister touched her swollen cheek. "I don't think it will do any good at this point. This is from Friday."

Ashley lifted her own shirt to inspect where the bullet had hit the vest. A huge bruise had already appeared, the surface puffy and tender to the touch.

Melissa stared at it with wide eyes. "What's that from?"

"A bullet. But I was wearing a bulletproof vest."

"Thank God," Melissa breathed.

She threw her arms around her sister's neck and clung to her for a moment. "Mel… I thought you might be dead."

Melissa hugged her tightly. "I know," she said, her voice choked. "It was awful. Thank God for Jeremy or I might be."

She gave her sister a kiss on the cheek and left her to finish cleaning up. Jeremy stood in the living room, looking uncomfortable.

"Thanks for saving my sister," she said.

His eyes skipped around the room, and she thought he looked guilty.

Melissa reappeared.

"Are you guys hungry? There's not much here, but I can make you something."

"Yeah, I'm famished."

She headed to the kitchen with Melissa and Jeremy trailing her. "So talk," she said, reaching into the cupboard and pulling out a couple of cans of chicken meat, a jar of mayonnaise, and a Cajun spice mix. "I think there's a jar of pickles in the fridge," she said, looking at Jeremy.

He opened the refrigerator door and pulled it out.

"So I met these two guys Thursday night at work," Melissa said, glancing at Jeremy, who Ashley thought looked guilty once again. Melissa worked as the manager of a trendy bar/nightclub in Colorado Springs. "They invited me to an after-party when we closed up, so I went."

Ashley listened as she opened the two cans of meat and scooped them into a bowl, mixing in the mayonnaise.

"So we partied for a while and then—"

"Wait," Ashley interrupted. "Was he one of them?" she asked, looking at Jeremy.

"Yeah. So the house party ends and Jeff, the other guy, invites me back to his place—with both of them," she said, blushing.

Ashley blushed too, knowing the two-men thing was her sister's top fantasy. She ducked her head to hide it and pulled some pickles out of the jar Jeremy had handed her. She picked up a knife and started chopping them.

"But he drove us to this nasty warehouse instead, and a bunch of guys with guns were there."

"Wait a minute," Ashley, said, whirling and pointing the tip of the knife at Jeremy. "*You* kidnapped my sister?" She took a menacing step forward, glaring at him.

He held his palms out. "I didn't know what was going on. Jeff is a friend—not even that good of a friend. I don't know why he brought me along."

"Probably because you're better with the ladies," Melissa muttered wryly.

A sound came from the living room and Ben appeared in wolf form. His lips curled up in a ferocious snarl when he saw Jeremy.

Melissa screamed and Jeremy froze, the whites of his eyes showing.

Ben growled, advancing toward Jeremy slowly.

Jeremy backed up until he hit the counter, cornered by the huge wolf.

"Is that a dog?" Melissa whispered.

She hesitated. She wanted to tell Melissa everything, but not in front of Jeremy. "Um, yeah, he's my friend Zolla's dog. I don't think he likes Jeremy. Easy, boy," she said to Ben, who showed no sign of backing off. "He helped Melissa escape, although I think he also kidnapped her, so maybe you should bite him," she said.

"What? Jesus!" Jeremy said, his face pale. "Get him away from me."

"Come, Wolfie," she said, walking toward the kitchen door and patting her thigh. She doubted Ben would comply, but she didn't know what else to do. "Come, boy. Is your master here?" she asked meaningfully.

Ben backed toward her, keeping his eye on Jeremy, his teeth still bared.

She tugged on the loose skin at his nape to turn him away.

"Be careful," Melissa gasped.

"It's okay," she said, pulling with all her weight. "He won't hurt me." Even though she believed it, when the huge animal turned abruptly, she jumped back out of his way. He gave one baleful look over his shoulder before heading toward Zolla's bedroom.

At the same time, she heard a car pull into the driveway.

She followed Ben, watching as he shifted gracefully back into human form, his naked body riddled with bullet wounds that only bled slightly, his cock jutting out at full mast.

"Ben," she cried, emotion flooding her. She ran and threw herself at him.

He looked surprised, but wrapped her up in his arms and pressed his lips to her hair. "Are you okay?" he asked.

She nodded against his chest. "Are you?"

"Yes." He pulled away to look at her, holding the back of her head, looking down at her with an intensity that made her shift in place. "Ashley, you disobeyed me."

The word *disobeyed,* combined with the burn of his dark gaze, made butterflies take flight in her stomach. The emotional turmoil of the entire meeting came flooding back. Pressure built behind her face, tears threatening. No words came to her lips.

"We'll talk about it later," he said meaningfully.

She gulped. Did that mean a spanking? Her pussy clenched even as fear turned her hands clammy.

"Where did you find your sister?"

She gathered her wits. "She called me as I was driving away from the bus station. She said Jeremy helped her escape. I haven't heard the full story yet."

"All right, let's get it now," he said, turning away and yanking on his jeans over his still enormous erection.

"Does that always happen when you shift?" she asked, eyeing his cock.

"No," he muttered. "Just around you."

She bit her lip to hide her smile.

Ben pulled on a t-shirt as the sound of the front door opening reached them. "Come on," he said, leading her back to the kitchen where she found Zolla drawing a gun on Jeremy. Apparently, he had the same instincts as Ben.

Jeremy's hands shot in the air. "Whoa, take it easy, man. We're with Ashley."

Zolla tipped the muzzle in Melissa's direction. "*She's* with Ashley. Who are you?"

"Are you Ben Stone?" Melissa squeaked.

"No, I am," Ben said, pushing through from behind Zolla to stand in front of Jeremy. "Who are you?"

ASHLEY'S SISTER'S face crumpled and she started to cry and he regretted his lack of finesse. The punk named Jeremy reached for her, drawing her against his side and Ben relaxed by a small measure. The two had clearly forged a genuine connection, whatever had happened between them.

"It's okay, Melissa," he said. "Why don't you come into the living room, sit down, and tell us your story?"

"I'll bring the food in," Ashley said, pushing through the crowded doorway to where she had some kind of food preparation going on the counter.

"Yeah, all right," Melissa said.

The group stepped into the living room, and Melissa told her story about being picked up by Jeremy and his friend, and delivered to some other thugs. It seemed Jeremy hadn't known what was going on, and when he realized and tried to get her out of it, he became as much of a prisoner as she. They spent three nights in an old barn out between Denver and Colorado Springs. According to Jeremy, his friend was given the order to kill him that afternoon, but had set him free instead, and he had circled back to save Melissa before they took her into Denver for the meetup. The two had hitchhiked into the city.

He and Zolla questioned them for over an hour until Ashley touched his shoulder. "Ben, please. I think they've told you everything they know. I'm sure Melissa could use a hot shower and a comfortable bed right now."

"They can stay here," Zolla offered, "if you think he's okay," he said, nodding toward Jeremy.

Ben glowered at Jeremy, but eventually lifted his shoulders. "He did the right thing in the end, I guess."

"The couch is a pull-out bed, and you two can have my bed," Zolla said, looking at Ben. "I can sleep on the floor."

He knew Ashley probably wanted to be with her sister, but after the fear of losing her that night, he just needed to hold her. "Ashley and I will get a motel nearby. Melissa and Jeremy can stay here on the sofa bed—just until we get the rest of this cleared up and we know it's safe for Ashley and Melissa to go to their homes."

Ashley stood up without a protest.

Zolla shrugged. "Of course. My place is yours for as long as you need it."

"Thank you," he said. He didn't understand why the wolf seemed so inclined to help him, but he wasn't in a position to argue with it. He needed all the help he could get.

BEN SAT on the edge of the motel bed, resting his forearms on his knees and his head in his hands. He'd taken off his belt and laid it beside him, but he wasn't sure he would actually go through with punishing Ashley. She was human, after all. It wasn't part of her culture to resolve things in a physical manner. Still, if she was to be his mate...

But she couldn't be, could she?

And even though she seemed to enjoy a little dominance from him, that didn't mean she would stand for a full-on spanking. Hell, he didn't even know if he could stand giving her one—the thought of hurting her made his stomach turn to lead. How did male wolves actually discipline their mates? Wasn't it their role to protect?

But it was exactly for that reason—because her disobedience made it harder to protect her—that he needed to be sure she learned this lesson.

She came out of the bathroom and stopped, looking over at him. "What are you thinking about?"

He sighed. "You and I have some unfinished business to discuss."

She drew a slow breath, obviously expecting this. She stood where she was, looking at him warily.

"I specifically told you to go straight to the car and drive away. Did you obey me?"

"I—" She stopped, as if realizing excuses or defenses were fruitless. "No, sir," she said softly.

Her use of the word *sir* gave him confidence to go on—she accepted his authority. "Because you were in danger, I could think of nothing but protecting you. I lost my game and some of them got away with the laptop."

She sucked in her breath. "I'm sorry." Her eyes flitted to his belt on the bed beside him. "Are you going to use that on me?"

"I haven't decided yet. What do you think I should do, Ashley?" He wanted her compliance.

She lifted her slender shoulders. "You're the boss," she whispered.

He figured that was as much consent as he would get. She wasn't going to ask him to spank her. He was the alpha; it was his duty to take charge. "Take off your clothes," he said, putting the edge of command into his voice.

Her cheeks colored, but she began to undress almost immediately, unzipping the wrinkled skirt and letting it drop to a puddle at her feet. She pulled the t-shirt over her head, then opened the back clasp of her bra, her breasts springing free. They were perfectly shaped, round and lifted, pale with peach nipples, which jutted out in eager points. An angry bruise stood out over her sternum, where a bullet had hit her vest. He tensed at the sight of it, his body ready to shift and fight to protect her. But the mark underlined the need for this discussion.

His jeans became too tight in the crotch area. He kept his face impassive. "Panties, too," he said, clearing his voice.

She hooked her thumbs in the waistband and lowered them over her thighs, bending to remove them.

When she straightened, fully naked, he suppressed a growl.

She slid her hands up and down her thighs, and then, as if suddenly aware of what she was doing, shook her hands out, but not before he caught the tremble in her fingers.

"Come here," he said.

She took a few steps toward him, but stopped, out of reach. He smelled the metallic scent of fear, mingled with the heady perfume of her arousal.

"Ashley," he said with a steely note of warning. "Come here."

She swallowed but did not move, her eyes darting to the belt on the bed once more.

"I know you're scared. Do you trust me to punish you?"

She caught his gaze, her blue eyes searching his. He knew she had no reason to trust him, but he held his breath for her answer.

She licked her lips and nodded, closing the distance between them.

The warmth of her trust spread through his body. Opening his knees, he grasped her hips and pulled her to stand between them. Her lips parted, her sternum rose and fell rapidly.

The conflict within him tore at his chest. *His to protect.* What if she cried? Would he be able to go on? He doubted it. He grit his teeth. Better to deal with this situation directly and have it over with. He pulled her face down over one knee and clamped his other leg over hers to keep her from kicking. Lifting his palm, he brought it down on one cheek, then the other. She gasped at first, but otherwise made no sound or protest. He spanked her with enough force to leave hand prints on her creamy flesh. She offered up her submission as easily as she'd given her whole self to him—placing herself in his hands with a trust he didn't deserve.

He continued with the punishment, slapping her cheeks until they turned rosy.

She had begun to wriggle and make little cries with each loud smack, but she still hadn't offered any resistance. As he paddled, her bottom bounced, cheeks flattening and springing back. Her pussy glistened between her legs, dewy with moisture. He wanted to stop spanking and drag his thumb over her glossy slit. He wanted to pleasure her with his fingers and his tongue.

But, no. Punishment first. And even if her body did respond to his dominance, that didn't necessarily mean she would be in the mood after he had spanked her raw.

He stopped and ran his hand over her heated buttocks. He hadn't expected her to take the spanking so well. He lifted her from his knees and stood with her, his body tight against hers.

She brought her hands to his chest.

Not yet.

"Go stand in the corner."

She lifted her startled gaze to meet his eyes. Obviously, she had thought the punishment was over.

"This is a lesson I'm serious about you learning, baby," he said. "Show me obedience," he said, lifting his chin toward the corner.

"Yes, sir," she said, blushing and dropping her gaze.

As he watched her walk to the corner, the evidence of his dominance standing out red against her pale skin, he felt a surge of some strong emotion. Love, maybe. Pride, that she had submitted to him, a desire to protect and care for her, yes, still the need to claim her, but for once, that took a back seat to the rest.

She faced the wall as he had directed, her pretty bottom painted red, her head bowed, juices leaking onto her inner thighs. He left her standing for no more than two minutes before he called her back.

"Come," he said.

She turned, looking more vulnerable than he'd seen her look before and his heart surged again to protect her. She walked over to him.

"Bend over, Ash," he said, pointing at the bed.

She looked over, her gaze flitting across his face, the line between her brows creased. He waited. Slowly, she folded her torso over the bed.

"Good girl."

He wrapped the buckle end of the belt around his hand until only about eighteen inches of length remained. Picking up her wrists, he pinned them at her low back with one of his hands. "I require your obedience at all times, Ashley," he said and swung the belt. The whoosh of displaced air sounded the moment before the leather struck her bare skin.

She yelped.

He stopped, trying to judge if it had been too hard or soft.

"I'm sorry, Ben," she squeaked.

"Thank you for your apology," he said, bringing the belt down again, and then a third time. She gasped with each blow, but did not protest. He whipped her, slowly and deliberately, setting a cadence of slaps and silences, punctuated by her little cries that grew louder with each stroke. Ashley buried her face in the covers.

He laid down five more and then dropped the belt, releasing her wrists.

When she jumped to her feet, he thought she was going to hightail it away from him, but instead she danced around, rubbing her bottom with a pained wince.

It was so cute, he had to bite back a smile and when she caught it, she flung herself at him. Her arms looped around his neck, her lips crushed against his.

He caught her up in surprise, pulling her body against his, squeezing the hot flesh of her ass. Kissing her back, he invaded her mouth with his tongue, claiming it. The animal in him roared to life, his cock swelling. Reason began to flee his mind.

Her fingers came to the hem of his shirt and she pulled it up, starting to peel it off him.

"What are you doing?" he croaked, trying to regain control.

She pulled back, frowning. "Don't you dare push me away again, Ben Stone," she said. "Not after everything that's happened," she said. The tears that hadn't come during the spanking now popped into her eyes, causing his heart to constrict painfully.

Of course, she was right. How could he deny her the closeness she craved when she'd just surrendered to him, mind, body, and soul?

"Ashley," he murmured, his body already painfully close to marking her. "Ashley…" He was trying to think of some words to explain why he couldn't give her what she seemed to need, but his body had another idea entirely. He had already yanked her against him, her soft, naked form melding to his.

She wrapped her legs around his waist, her naked pussy hot against his belly. He walked her to the bed and laid her on her back where he bit and sucked his way down her neck to her left breast.

"Fuck me, Ben," she begged in a guttural tone.

"I can't," he managed to croak, crawling down

between her thighs. He spread her knees up and licked into her.

The taste of her arousal hit him like a bolt of lightning, a shock shuddering through his body, screaming at him to claim her.

Mark her. Mark her now.

Her fingers twined in his hair, pulling it roughly as she rolled her pelvis up and down, sliding her slit over his tongue.

She yanked his hair. "Why won't you fuck me?"

"I don't want to hurt you, Ash," he managed to say, sliding two fingers inside her to distract her.

The walls of her vagina tightened immediately around his fingers, clenching. He shoved them up further, seeking her sweet spot. Finding it, he curled his fingers to stroke it, feeling the tissue thicken under his fingertips.

"I know you're huge, but I think I'll stretch," she panted.

He choked back a laugh. "You think I'm huge? No, don't answer—that's not what I meant. It's… wolves are rough, really rough."

She moaned wantonly and he closed his eyes. Her scent filled his nostrils, taking over all his senses. He needed to cool down or he would lose control and mark her.

But Ashley was rocking her little pelvis, thrusting her breasts toward the ceiling. Her willing submission to both his punishment and his pleasure made her undeniably *his*. His need to please and protect her, to cherish her, to care for her in every way rose up so fiercely it almost blinded him.

Heat suffused his body, not the heat of the shift to mark her, but of something else. Something deeper and more emotional. He had never in his life acted with anyone else's needs ahead of his.

His dad had modeled selfishness, and he'd followed suit. Leon had gone the opposite direction, caring for his hundreds of employees, his pack, and his family, all without complaint. Now, as he watched his female flushing with pleasure, her sensuous mouth falling open on a moan, he knew he'd do anything for her—even if he never found satisfaction himself. Giving her pleasure had become more important than receiving.

He circled her clit with his thumb as he continued to slowly penetrate her with two fingers, then three.

"Turn over," he instructed.

She rolled to her belly, looking over her shoulder at him with glassy eyes. He found her slit from behind and slid inside with his two fingers, working his thumb against the little rosette of her back hole. She cried out, the muscles of her pussy clenching around his fingers.

He gathered some of her natural lubricant on his thumb and circled her anus, massaging the quivering hole as he continued to push in and out of her pussy.

"Please," she whimpered, humping the bed.

He pushed more insistently on her anus. "Open for me," he ordered, the timbre of command threading his voice. Her muscle relaxed and he breached the entrance. Massaging around the opening, he entered her to one knuckle, then the next.

She cried out, arching back like a bow. He finger-fucked her, rocking his fingers between her back hole and her pussy. When she began to thrash against him, he thrust harder, somehow miraculously able to keep his mind off his own body's reaction.

Sliding his free hand underneath her, he rubbed her clit. She came, her entire body bucking, her internal muscles squeezing his fingers in a pulsing release. He groaned, his cock throbbing painfully for release. He continued to pump into both her holes until her muscles relaxed and she collapsed in a limp heap beneath him.

"Oh, wow," she breathed.

He eased his fingers out of her, trying not to think about how badly he wanted to take her with brutal force.

She rolled over and gazed up at him, a contented smile playing on her lips. "Why do you do that?"

"What?"

She blushed. "You know. Put your finger there."

He grinned at her embarrassment. "Because I like to see you come undone."

She flushed a little more.

He leaned over and grazed one nipple with his teeth. "Little girl, if I ever have to punish you for putting yourself in danger again, I will put more than my finger there. I will fuck your ass with my big, hard cock until you see stars."

"Oh, God," she cried, reaching down to clutch her pussy as her hips bucked in another orgasm.

ASHLEY WOKE with Ben's considerable erection still pressing into her back, just as it had when he'd lain down beside her the night before. He wore his clothes while she lay completely naked, which seemed to be the metaphor for their entire relationship.

She squeezed her bottom, trying to see if it was still sore. Not at all. Why did that disappoint her? She remembered Ben's punishment with a flutter of her belly. As strange as it may seem, she loved when he got stern with her, and she loved that he punished her physically. He was the embodiment of every fantasy she'd ever had.

Melissa had always told her she liked authority figures. Ashley had gone moony over male teachers and coaches in her teen years, and had full-on crushes on several professors in college. It only stood to reason she would fall head over heels with her hot boss when she entered the workplace. And he was so much more than a hot boss. He was an alpha wolf—stern, dominant, and sexy in every way. And he took her to task.

She knew every red flag should be flying over the fact that he'd taken a belt to her ass—not for kinky pleasure, but for an actual punishment—but she had loved it. Well, she hadn't loved the pain when she was in the middle of it, but she loved that he had done it and that the threat of future punishment dangled over her head. Besides, she was fairly certain he would have stopped if she'd told him no. There seemed to be a moment there when he had been looking for her consent. And he'd seemed saddened or troubled beforehand—he hadn't lashed out in anger, it had been more like he faced a difficult, but necessary task. He would make a good leader if he ever chose to be alpha to his pack.

From what she had deduced, the other wolves were disappointed in his reluctance to step forward. They wanted to follow him, and she understood why. He possessed sheer power of presence and mind. If only he believed in his own ability to lead.

She rolled over and he adjusted in his sleep to keep her in his arms, tucked against his muscled torso. She still owed him for last night. She'd drifted to sleep while he'd lain beside her with probably the world's worst case of blue balls.

She slipped out of bed to go to the bathroom, then returned with a condom. She didn't engage in casual sex, but Melissa's last boyfriend had stuffed a bunch in her purse as a joke a while back and she'd never taken them out. Now she was grateful she had them. She sat beside Ben and ran her hand over his arm, marveling at the definition of his biceps. Sliding her palm down his side, she slipped it under his shirt, feeling the heat of his golden skin.

He stirred, reaching for her and pulling her back down beside him without opening his eyes. As if she belonged there. She smiled and tugged on the button on his jeans, working it open. Sliding down, out of his grasp, she straddled his legs and unzipped his pants. He didn't wear boxers or briefs—probably with all the shifting back and forth it wasn't worth the hassle. Didn't wearing underwear make men's sperm count lower anyway? As if Ben Stone needed to be more virile. Regardless, it made it easier for her to free his length, which sprang out with its impressive size.

She gripped the base and squeezed and he groaned, shifting in his sleep and mumbling something. She lowered her lips to taste him. The moment she put her mouth over the head, his eyes sprang open. His cock also seemed to double in size, which she hadn't believed possible. She licked under the rim, all the way around, as Ben stared down with a startled expression. A drop of pre-cum emerged and she lapped it up with her tongue, then licked her lips while holding his gaze.

A shudder ran through his entire body. Satisfied with her results, she closed her lips around his shaft and lowered her head over it. Her jaw felt way too small, but she did her best to relax her gag reflex and take him deep into her throat.

He made a sound as if in pain.

She did it again.

His face twisted, eyes never leaving her face. "Ashley—" he groaned.

"Mmm hmm," she said, keeping her mouth over his length and humming her response, knowing the vibration would drive him mad.

Like the first time she'd sucked his cock, he gripped the headboard, as if afraid to touch her.

"Why are you doing this?" he croaked.

She smiled and released his cock from her mouth. "I want you to feel good," she purred, then dragged her tongue from his balls up the underside of his cock to the frenulum, where she swirled her tongue again.

"Ohh," he groaned.

"Does it?" she asked.

"What?" he grunted.

"Feel good?"

"No! Yes, Oh, God. Ahhh-uh… it's too much. It's too fucking good."

Encouraged, she took him deep into her throat again.

"Noo." He sounded pained again.

"No?" she asked innocently, sitting up. She ripped open the condom wrapper and rolled it down his cock before he could ask what she was doing.

She understood he was worried about being too rough with her, but she wanted to give herself to him. And while she'd never had a rough lover before, it sounded delicious. She moved quickly to straddle him.

"No, no, no, no," he said, lifting her hips off and holding her pelvis suspended in the air.

"Ben," she said in her sexiest voice. "I need you inside me. I need you inside me now."

His cock strained to reach her, enormous, thick and pulsing, just inches from her pussy.

A drip of her arousal fell onto it and he inhaled sharply. His green eyes flickered to amber once, twice, then they stayed yellow, an inhuman growl emerging from his throat. He yanked her down, impaling her with his cock. Even as ready as she was for him, his size stretched her wide, sending tears of pain springing to her eyes.

She cried out, struggling to adjust to the suddenness of the invasion, but he was already pushing and pulling her hips forward and back. Her clit rubbed over the base of his cock, sending shocks of pleasure shooting down her inner thighs and curling her toes. Her pussy emitted a fresh gush of moisture, easing the stretch so she could take him deeper.

She moaned, arching into his hands. His fingers tightened on her hips. Another growl passed his lips and he yanked her harder and faster. She gave herself over to him, knowing any resistance might cause her pain. Her muscles went limp, as if she'd already orgasmed, relaxing to let him move her like a rag doll.

His lip curled and he snarled, the pads of his fingers digging into her ass as he thrust upward at the same time he yanked her forward.

She cried out, fresh tears stinging her eyes, although the pleasure by far outweighed the pain.

In a single motion, he lifted her completely off his cock, flipped her onto her belly and pinned her down, straddling her legs. Another snarl reached her ears. He wrapped a fist in her hair, pulling her head back until she arched as he plowed deep into her channel. She felt like a virgin, stretched to the maximum, shocked by both the pain and the plea-sure of it all.

Ben slammed into her, over and over again with an urgency and violence that stunned her. Even so, her body wanted all of it, wanted more of it, until she'd raised her voice in a continuous, keening cry.

Ben's breath panted hot in her ear, his desperation for release evident in the way his hand tore the sheet beneath her, yanking even the mattress cover up with his effort to bury himself inside her.

He roared, his seed so hot she felt it, even through the condom.

And then a searing pain ripped through her shoulder, blinding her.

IT WAS the salty smell of her tears that jerked him back to his full human form. Her blood was in his mouth, her scream ringing in his ears. He released the grip of his jaws and reared back off her, horrified.

Blood ran down her back, soaking the bed.

He shouted in alarm, his voice mingling with her sobs. *Oh, no.* His heart rate shot to arrhythmic levels, palms turned cold and sweaty. "Ashley?" he croaked, his voice hoarse.

She had scrambled up, crouched in a ball at the head of the bed, her eyes wide with terror. He reached for her and she flinched.

"Don't touch me," she cried. Her lips trembled, tears streamed down her face, mingling with her blood on her collarbone.

Oh, God. *What had he done?*

He stumbled back, his limbs cold. "Ashley…"

She cowered, holding her hand up, as if to ward him away.

Hot tears filled his own eyes. "Please," he whispered, not even sure what he was begging for. *Don't hate me. Don't be seriously hurt.*

"Don't," she cried, pressing herself up against the wall as if she wanted to push herself right through it to get away from him.

"I won't," he said, a tear streaking his cheek as he backed up. "I won't touch you. I won't ever hurt you again." He turned and ran, throwing open the door and shifting without changing his clothes, which caused them to rip at the seams and fall off as he raced away.

He gulped the cool morning air, ignoring the occasional joggers who looked terrified at seeing a huge wolf race by. He ran fast and hard, with no destination in mind. He followed a creek bed and ran through parks, killing a goose just for sport.

When he found himself at Zolla's back door, he figured some better instinct must have crept in, and followed it inside. Bursting through the doggy door, he ran past where Melissa and Jeremy still lay on the fold-out couch. Zolla opened the bedroom door just as he reached it, probably hearing or smelling him.

He looked unsurprised by his arrival, as if he'd

been waiting for him to appear. "It's Jack," he announced the moment Ben shifted to human form. Zolla pointed to his computer screen at the IP address listed. "Every one of Stone's servers crashed fifteen minutes ago. Stone Gaming is completely down all over the world. I don't know what his plan is, but I do know for certain that computer that logged in with your password thirty minutes ago is registered to Jack Laden. Here's his address."

Ben snatched the paper and memorized the address.

"Is that blood on your face?" Zolla asked, sniffing the air.

He tried to breathe and failed. "Yeah," he managed to say. Knowing her sister was in the other room and would also hate him for what he'd done only increased his shame. "I marked her. It's bad. Really bad. I need you to go to her." It was a sign of his desperation that he would send another male to take care of his mate.

Zolla's jaw dropped, but he thankfully didn't comment. "Where?"

He gave him the name of the motel and the room number. "You'll go now?"

"Of course. Where are you going?"

"To take care of Jack."

"You shouldn't go alone. Call Mark or wait for me."

He shook his head. "No, I can handle him. You

just make sure Ashley—" he swallowed. "Just go to her. Now."

Zolla pulled on a Rockies cap. "I'm leaving."

Ben shifted back to wolf form and followed Zolla out, taking off for the place he'd hidden his car Friday night. Using the hidden button to pop his trunk, he rummaged in the duffel bag for a pair of pants, shirt, and shoes. With the spare key, he started the car up and drove toward the address of Jack's foothill residence. His mind was blank—or rather, held only clear focus of intent: eliminate Jack. After he dealt with him, he would open the box in which he'd stuffed his anguish over Ashley.

He parked in front of an ostentatious house with a cobblestone driveway and a giant fountain in the front. Getting out, he stalked up the sidewalk. He tried the door first, and finding it locked, slammed his shoulder against the heavy wood. The wood bowed against his shifter strength. He threw his weight into it again, then a third time, cracking the door from the hinges.

It swung open and he found himself face to face with Jack, who pointed a revolver at him.

Ben spread his hands. "What's your plan, Jack?" he asked, stepping in and swinging the broken door shut behind him.

Jack's nostrils flared, his little eyes darting past Ben toward the door.

"You planted a bomb in my laptop, but haven't

triggered it yet. You kidnapped Ashley's sister. You just toppled every one of our servers. Are you trying to lower our stock so you can buy it all out with me out of the picture? Do you think Shayla would let you do that?"

Jack's face had gone pale, that muscle under his right eye twitched as it always did when he challenged Ben. The hand holding the revolver shook slightly, but his expression was all sneer.

Ben advanced slowly. "The FBI knows all about the kidnapping and the bomb," he said, only partly bluffing. Mark knew, after all, so if or when things came out with the authorities, Mark would see that the right people were prosecuted and any references to wolves were left out. "They already traced the server crash to your IP address."

Jack fired the gun, hitting him in the gut.

Ben did his best not to flinch, despite the burn, and gave a mirthless laugh, his upper lip curling. He walked casually forward as if the bullet didn't bother him. "Who are you working with? The Sandoval cartel?"

Jack gaped, his eyes dropping to the bleeding wound, then back to Ben's face. The sneer faded, confusion creeping in. "I don't know who that is." He fired again, this time hitting Ben right in the sternum.

He lost his breath, but he did not stagger backward. "Who then?"

Jack's hand trembled violently as he finally comprehended that Ben couldn't be eliminated as easily as he had thought. "What are you?"

He grinned. "I can't be killed, Jack," he lied. "What does that do to your plans?"

Jack's eyes darted around the room and he began to back up.

"Your idea was clever, I'll admit that," he said, hoping to get him to talk. He needed to know who else was involved and what Jack's exact motivation had been. "And rather elaborate. Wouldn't it have been easier to just shoot me right from the beginning?"

Jack's eyes fell to the bullet wounds again. "Yeah, but I wanted the server crash to be on your watch."

"You wanted the board to fire me?"

His mouth twisted into a bitter grimace. "I wanted there to be nothing left of Stone Technologies," he spat. "So my stock options from the employment package at Suma Games would make me rich."

"You already are rich," he muttered, then shook his head. Why was he arguing with an insane man?

A bead of sweat dripped down Jack's face, but he gave a twisted grin. "It's nothing more than I deserve. I invented the NE3, not Leon."

A flash of irritation on Leon's behalf made him surge forward.

Jack fired again. This time it caught Ben in the ribs, well below his heart. The impact seared and momentarily knocked him back, but he kept his face blank and snatched the gun out of Jack's hands. Ben turned it around and smacked Jack on the head with the handle side.

Jack crumpled to the carpeted floor, groaning.

Ben kicked him in the ribs. "Hey, Jack—you're fired."

He flipped the gun back around, pointed it at the little weasel's head, and discharged it.

ASHLEY'S HEAD swam like she'd downed three margaritas on an empty stomach. The dizziness seemed different than weakness caused by blood loss—there was a pleasant, but disoriented sensation, too. She'd somehow managed to get dressed and held a towel to the puncture wounds, but blood had soaked through her shirt and the towel and the sight made her nauseous. Her emotions were a tangled mess, too. She couldn't stop crying—not because of the pain, although it was still excruciating, but more from shame and betrayal. Why had he bitten her? She had trusted him, given herself to him, and he'd turned savage. Had she somehow angered him? Surely tearing a hunk out of her shoulder wasn't what he meant when he said wolves were rough when they had sex. Or was that the 'marking' she'd heard them talk about? Was this why he'd been so afraid to have sex with her?

Maybe so, but why had he just abandoned her afterward? He'd walked out the door while she'd been huddled naked and bleeding and he hadn't returned. Even as she swore she'd never forgive him for this, her lovesick heart kept waiting for him to return and explain himself. But he hadn't.

A tap sounded on the door.

She froze. Ben wouldn't knock. Who could it be?

"Ashley? It's Zolla. Ben sent me over to help you. Can you let me in?"

He sent Zolla? She felt queasy. She didn't even merit him coming himself? She stood up from where she'd been sitting on the edge of the bed and wobbled over to open the door.

Zolla took in the bloodied towel without surprise. He stepped through the door and closed it quickly behind him. Pulling out a chair, he pointed at it. "May I look at your wounds?"

"Where's Ben?" she asked as she found her way to the indicated chair.

"He went after Jack."

That made her even angrier. Clearly, she meant nothing to him—he'd pawned her off on his friend while he went for revenge. It seemed he had only been keeping her around to make the trade with his laptop. She'd been a fool to think he had any feelings for her.

Zolla tore her shirt open at the neckline to expose her shoulder.

"Hey," she protested. "You could've just asked me to take it off. This is the only shirt I have at the moment, you know."

"Yeah, I'm not going to answer to Ben for having your shirt off," he muttered.

"Ben has no claim on me," she said bitterly.

Zolla raised his eyebrows and pursed his lips as if to show he disagreed, but wasn't going to argue. He inspected the punctures in her skin and then walked to the bathroom where he wet a washcloth in the sink. When he returned, he cleaned the wounds.

She drew a breath. "Why did he do this to me? Is… is this what wolves do when they have sex?"

"No. He marked you. Do you know what that means?"

She shook her head, then stopped, wincing as the pain shot across her trapezius muscle.

"I don't think he meant to do it, but his instinct probably took over. It means he's chosen you as his mate. When a shifter male marks his mate, a special secretion coats his teeth. You probably feel a little drugged right now?"

"Yeah," she said.

"The secretion is embedded in your flesh and

his scent remains permanently, telling other wolves you are taken by him."

A flood of indignation soaked through her. How dare he permanently mark her? She would be scarred for life and he hadn't even asked first. And then he'd just walked out on her and sent Zolla over like she was some mess someone else had to clean up.

"This is bullshit," she said, twisting to glare at Zolla, as if it was his fault his pack mate was an asshole. "He just bites a chunk out of my shoulder and then disappears and sends you to clean it up? Can you get his scent out of me, because I am sure as hell not sticking around for this kind of treatment."

Zolla had leaned in close to inspect the marks under her collarbone. "Ashley... do you always heal this fast?" he asked.

"What do you mean?" She stood up and walked to the bathroom to look in the mirror. The gashes that had been so horrible forty-five minutes before had mostly closed, the bleeding stopped.

"I don't know," she said. "Is this fast?"

Zolla waited for her to return. "Yes. Most humans would require multiple stitches and would still be bleeding freely, but your blood has already coagulated and the flesh is sticking together as if this wound were a day old, instead of an hour."

She touched her shoulder, trying to understand what he was telling her.

"Do you have any shifter blood in the family?"

She gaped at him. "You mean…?" Her mind raced, instantly arriving on Grandma Jane, who had given birth to her dad out of wedlock. It had been a scandalous family secret, and her father had been raised believing Abe Bell, his stepfather, was his real father until he saw his own birth certificate when he went off to college. The line for father had been filled in as 'unknown.' He'd confronted his mother and she'd refused to tell him anything, other than that Abe Bell loved him as his own and that was all that mattered.

Had Grandma Jane had a fling with a shifter?

Ashley considered how her father had always bragged that neither he nor his daughters ever got sick. It was true, their mother had her share of colds and flus, but Ashley and Melissa rarely caught anything, and when they did, it was mild in comparison to other people's.

"Maybe I do heal fast," she said slowly, remembering times when she or Melissa thought they'd sprained something only to have the swelling and pain be gone by morning. "I think I just always thought I was lucky."

"It would explain Ben's fascination with you."

She narrowed her eyes. "What do you mean?"

He waved his hands as if to ward off her

temper. "I didn't mean any offense by that. You're gorgeous and smart, anyone can see that, it's just that alphas don't usually choose humans as their mates. Biology would demand they choose the strongest or most suitable female for breeding."

She sniffed, her anger with Ben returning full force.

"Listen… it's none of my business, but—" He broke off when she whirled to glare at him.

"What?" she demanded.

"Just—don't be too hard on him. He looked about as miserable as I've ever seen him this morning. I don't think he meant to hurt you and I know he felt terrible about it."

Some of her anger lessened, which for some reason made her feel weepy. She drew in several breaths to get control. "Well, why in the hell did he leave?"

Zolla shrugged. "I don't know. My sense is that he carries around a lot of guilt—something to do with Leon's death. He feels responsible for some reason. And I think hurting someone else he loved just made him tuck tail and run."

Hearing that Zolla believed Ben loved her made her nose burn. She rubbed it.

"Honestly, Ashley. I know he didn't mean to hurt you."

She looked away to hide the emotion in her face.

His phone rang and he answered it. "How'd it go?" He listened for a moment. "Do you need cleanup?"

She strained her ears to hear the other person talking, wondering if it was Ben.

Her question was answered with Zolla's next reply. "She's okay. No major arteries, the wounds are healing well… No, she won't need to see a doctor, unless she wants to." He raised his eyebrows in question at her and she shook her head. "Okay." Zolla held out the phone to her. "He wants to talk to you."

She folded her arms across her chest and shook her head.

Zolla spoke into the phone. "Hey, man, she's not feeling up to it, yet." He turned away as if having a private conversation with Ben. "Give her a little time. It was a little shocking for her, that's all."

"A *little?*" she muttered.

Zolla hung up and turned back to her. "He thinks it's safe for you and Melissa to return home."

"What happened with Jack?"

"Ben took care of him. He had taken a job at Suma Games and wanted to ruin Stone and steal the code before he left."

"What did Ben do?"

"He finished it," he said with a finality that made her shiver. "He thinks it's safe for you and Melissa to go home now."

Though it was irrational, disappointment at once again being dissed by Ben sent bile into her throat. "Great," she said in a strangled voice. "Is Mel still at your place?"

"Yeah, I'll head back and let her know. Do you want her to call you or anything?"

"Tell her to meet me at my place," she said, picking up her purse and fishing out the keys.

"Will do," Zolla said, opening the door and waiting for her to go through it first.

"Thanks," she said, turning and giving Zolla a hug.

He froze, patting her awkwardly on the back. He cleared his throat. "Uh, no problem. You shouldn't need to put anything on that bite—no hydrogen peroxide or antibiotic. The serum will protect you from infection. Are you okay to drive or do you still feel drugged?"

"I'm okay to drive," she said. She felt odd, but the vertigo had worn off. "Is it okay to get it wet? I could use a long shower."

"Should be fine. Just take it easy today. Put my number in your phone and call me if you have any questions or if you feel worse. Or if you need anything."

She entered him into her contacts and gave him a weak smile. "Thanks again, Zolla."

"Yeah. Be kind to your wolf, Ashley. He really is sorry."

She shrugged. "He has yet to tell me that." *Not that she'd given him the opportunity.*

She was grateful that Zolla didn't point out that would have been impossible since she'd refused to take Ben's call. She knew she was being somewhat irrational, but Ben's abandonment was the clincher in a whole string of emotional shut-outs from the very beginning of their relationship.

She'd had enough. She didn't know where they'd be going from here, but she was damn sure she wasn't going to let it continue like this. She couldn't go on feeling this unsteady. She didn't give herself to a guy only to have him vanish every time things got intense.

10

That afternoon, Ben sat in his office, the quiet deafening. Zolla had come to consult with Ben's IT guys to get all the servers back up and running and the security back in place.

His stomach stayed in knots all day thinking about Ashley. The fact that she didn't take his call provided a fresh source of torture. He tried again several times, but each time it went straight to voicemail, as if she'd shut her phone off or her battery was dead.

He prayed she wasn't suffering. He had doubts about how well Zolla had cared for her. Maybe he should've insisted she be taken into emergency for stitches. Had she been given any painkillers? Would she ever speak to him again?

As he walked out to his car, he tried her again. Once more it went straight to voicemail. He hadn't left a message the other times, but he made an attempt. "Ashley," he said. His mind went blank. What the hell did you say in this situation? Was there a Hallmark card for this? *I'm sorry I almost tore your throat out, will you be my valentine?* Or maybe *I'm ready to go to the next step with you... do you mind if I permanently scar your flesh to embed my scent?* No, even better, *I'd like to endanger you by making sure all my enemies know I care. Hope you don't mind the scarring.*

Damn. He was really the biggest asshat, wasn't he?

He drew a breath and exhaled. "Please call me. I really need to talk to you. I—I'm sorry, Ashley. I need to see you..." He started to say *please call me,* but realizing he'd already said that, hit 'end,' and rubbed his forehead.

What if she didn't call? Should he show up at her house? Or wait to see her at work? God, would she even come to work? The thought of running Stone without her left him empty. In less than a week, she had become his everything. Because of her, he wanted to fix Stone, he wanted to man up and be the leader his brother had expected him to be. Leon deserved that. Ashley somehow had woken him up from the stupor he'd been in since his brother's death.

He got in his car and drove to her house. The lights were on and he could see Ashley and Melissa sitting together on the sofa. He sat with the car idling for a moment, considering. Both women probably had a lot to share with each other. Maybe it was better to let them lick their wounds together without him interrupting.

He put the Mustang back in gear and drove home.

TURNING off her phone when she was angry with Ben for abandoning her rivaled cutting off her nose to spite her face. Probably some part of her wanted to punish him. And maybe the other just wasn't ready to talk. She needed to sort out her feelings about the whole 'marking' thing.

By the time she had told the entire story to Mel, she'd begun to feel the magnitude of it all. It wasn't just about being shocked over the violence or angry over the abandonment. Ben had forever marked her as his mate. She had to admit her heart did a giddy dance when she realized the implications. She'd been right—he did have a thing for her. A serious thing, by the sounds of it. She didn't know what it meant to be a wolf's mate, but if they could work past the walls Ben put up, she sure as hell wanted to give it a try.

She had turned her phone back on before she went to bed, and was satisfied to hear Ben's message. He'd sounded terrible. She still hadn't been ready to talk to him, but she felt a lot better. Today, she could face him at work. They would talk and could move forward from there.

She drove in early and found a place in the garage close to the elevator. "Hang on," she called out as the elevator doors shut on a man she didn't recognize. She shoved her hand between the doors to open them and slid in. "Thirty-fifth floor, please," she said.

He pressed the button without looking at her. She took in his shiny shoes first, then his crisp, clean designer business suit. He had dark hair, graying at the temples, and olive skin, darker than Ben's. His eyes met hers and he wrinkled his nose as he sniffed the air.

She froze at the distinctly wolf-like gesture.

Her tension seemed to be the confirmation he needed because his lips curled into an ugly smile. "You've been freshly marked," he observed in a thick Spanish accent.

She jerked her gaze away and looked up at the illuminated floor numbers above the doors. "I don't know what you mean."

In one swift movement, he pulled a gun out of his jacket pocket and pointed it at her. "When the elevator reaches the destination, you will stay on, close the doors, and take it back down to the garage."

She held her breath, trying to organize her

thoughts. Who was this man? Someone from South America… Leon had died in Venezuela. What had Ben told her about it?

The doors opened and the gun disappeared into his jacket pocket, still pointed directly at her. "Close them. *Now*," he growled.

She hit the 'close door' button. The elevator continued up to Ben's floor. Please, she prayed, let him be out by Karen's desk where he would see her standing there with the wolf she presumed was his enemy.

No such luck. The doors slid open to an empty reception area. Karen wasn't at her desk, and Ben's door was closed.

"Close the doors and hit P1."

She hesitated.

"Do it!" he snarled.

She obeyed. "Who are you?"

The shifter's lip curled. "I am Sandoval."

She looked at him blankly.

"He has not told you about me?" he asked, sounding offended.

She shrugged, trying to look unconcerned.

"I am the wolf who's going to make your lover boy pay."

"What did he do to you?"

The doors slid open in the garage and the nasty wolf shoved her forward, out of the elevator. "Tomás Solís murdered my wife and children."

She sucked in her breath, the blast of hatred from the man almost palpable. She didn't know who Tomás Solís was, but she didn't think it was the right time to ask.

He marched her forward, his fingers on her upper arm digging into her flesh. Two younger men jumped out of a dark car and one of them held the door open for Sandoval. "Get in," he snapped, shoving her forward.

"Who's this?" one of the younger men asked. He resembled her captor—perhaps he was his son or nephew.

Sandoval pushed in to sit beside her. "The Solís pup's mate."

"What do we want with her?" the other man asked.

"Just drive the car," Sandoval snapped. "Back to the house."

The car backed out and sped out of the parking garage. She scanned the cars coming in, thinking she might try to flag down help, but she realized the windows were too tinted for anyone to see her inside.

The older wolf's son twisted around in the front seat to look at her, and then his father. He said something in Spanish.

The older man said something back, then turned to her, a nasty smile on his face.

"I killed Solís too fast. I should have made him

watch while I tortured his pups before his eyes." He picked up a lock of her hair and twirled it between his fingers. "But now I can rectify that." His dark eyes glinted. "His son can watch his mate defiled, then killed. And then, when I finish the youngest Solís, my vengeance will be complete."

Was Ben the youngest Solís?

"I-I'm not actually Ben's mate. It was a mistake —he didn't mean to mark me. I'm human."

"Which makes you all the more fragile." The man smiled. "Torturing a human is so rewarding."

She shuddered.

The car pulled up to a villa-style vacation rental —a self-contained unit, two stories high with a wall surrounding the property.

Terror had seeped in, turning her entire body cold. She took deep breaths, trying to keep her wits. She had her phone. Maybe she could find a way to text Ben or Zolla. Zolla might be able to trace her location.

Sandoval shoved her out of the car and pulled her into the house, sitting her down and taping her ankles to the legs of a chair. He taped her wrists behind her, so tight the wood from the chair dug into her arms. Rummaging in her purse, he pulled out her phone and scrolled through it. "Where is lover boy's number?" he asked, not seeming to expect an answer. "Ah, here it is." He hit dial on the number and held it to her ear. "Say hello to him."

Ben answered on the second ring. "Ashley," he croaked, sounding relieved. She remembered with a painful twist in her chest that they were at odds, and she hadn't returned his phone calls. Tears of regret stung her eyes.

"Ben—"

Sandoval took the phone away from her and said something in Spanish.

"Ben, don't come—it's a trap," she yelled.

Sandoval struck her with the back of his hand, slamming her head back. She tasted blood as pain exploded in her mouth, jaw, and neck.

"Don't come," she repeated, as Sandoval walked away with the phone, still speaking into it.

SANDOVAL HAD ASHLEY. Ben's vision domed, his senses razor-sharp. It took him only three seconds to determine his course of action. He called Zolla as he drove to the address Sandoval had given him.

"Are you crazy?" Zolla demanded. "You can't go in there alone—you'll never walk back out. Tell me where and I'll meet you."

"No. I'm going alone and unarmed, as instructed. I'm not taking any chances where Ashley's concerned." He hung up before Zolla could begin his arguments and pressed his foot down on the gas.

He pulled up at the address and stepped out of the car. For once, his mind was perfectly clear where Ashley was concerned. A strange peace had settled around him like a cloak, giving him a serene sense of power. He walked to the door and knocked.

The curtains moved and a shadow passed in front of the peephole of the door. It opened a crack and the butt of a gun emerged. *"Pásale."*

He stepped in and waited as he was patted down for a gun with his hands on his head. Two thugs from Sandoval's pack flanked him and walked him into the living room, where his female was bound to a chair. Seeing her like that—her face bruised, her eyes wide in a pale face—almost caused him to lose his calm determination.

"Ben," she whispered. "I told you not to come."

"It's going to be all right, Ashley," he promised. Hands still on his head, he walked forward and dropped to his knees before Sandoval.

His father's nemesis curled his lip, his eyes gleaming with satisfaction.

"Take me," he said. "Have your revenge—lord knows, you deserve it. But let her go."

Sandoval's face split into an ugly smile. "Look at this, Rodrigo, he's begging already, and we haven't even started."

Some of Ben's clarity chipped away. He shook his head, keeping his hands glued to it. "You don't have to prove anything," he promised the drug lord.

"I know you were wronged. I heard about what happened to your family," he said, referring to the deaths of Sandoval's wife and daughters. "If I could change the way things happened, I would. I would change a lot of my father's misdeeds."

Sandoval looked angry now, as if the very mention of Tomás Solís enraged him.

Ben plowed forward before Sandoval stopped him. "For what it's worth, I think it was an accident —that you were the intended target—but I honestly can't be sure. My father was a real asshole. He wanted you out of the picture, and he took the coward's path instead of just challenging you. He lost his honor and I'm not proud to be his son." His eyes traveled past Sandoval to his son, who sat beside him. "I didn't come to his aid when he called me back to fight you. But I will offer myself up now. Do not hurt Ashley. She has nothing to do with this."

Sandoval's smile fell away and he regarded Ben with a narrowed gaze. His son looked uncomfortable.

Ben would have appealed to Sandoval's honor, except the man had even fewer scruples than his father had. He glanced at Ashley, who had tears streaming down her face. She shook her head at him, as if trying to communicate that Sandoval could not be trusted.

Sandoval stood and walked toward him. "I lost

my wife and both my daughters because of you," he said.

"Not me," Ben said. "I wasn't even in the country. I didn't know anything about it."

Sandoval pointed a shaking finger at him. "You should've stopped him," he shouted.

Ben closed his eyes. Sandoval's sanity appeared to be slipping, which didn't bode well for his plan of sacrificing himself to save Ashley. "You're right," he said. "I should have. If I had known about it, I would have," he said, even though it was a lie. He had never stood up to his father, had only run away from the abusive and controlling parent.

Sandoval walked to Ashley and cut the tape from around her ankles, yanking her to her feet.

He tensed.

"I want you to suffer the way I have suffered. The way Mia and Sofi and Ana suffered." He bent Ashley over the table and lifted her skirt.

Ben tensed, his vision changing, a roar in his ears.

As if from a distance, he heard Sandoval saying, "You're going to watch while every one of us has his way with your woman and then you're going to watch her die."

Ben shifted before Sandoval had finished speaking, launching for his throat. Sandoval fired a bullet into the back of Ashley's calf and she screamed.

Two wolves met Ben's launch midair and brought him down, snarling.

"Freeze or she's dead," Sandoval shouted, the gun at Ashley's temple.

A second gunshot rang out at the same moment the glass in every window of the room broke. Ben leaped once more for Sandoval, but he already lay on the floor in a confusing pile of blood and bodies. Ashley was under him, screaming. Wolves were flying in through the windows, snarling and attacking the South American pack. He recognized Zolla and Mark, Stanley and others.

He tore Sandoval from Ashley and found him dead, shot through the back of his head. Crouching over Ashley to protect her, he bared his teeth and growled, but no threat came. Though jaws were still snapping and bodies still tussled, the Denver pack had taken control. A few moments later, they subdued the remaining South American wolves to whimpers and tucked tails.

He whimpered and licked Ashley's bloodied face. She moved her face away from him, but did not seem wholly conscious. His heart beat in his throat.

The wolves around him began to shift back to human form. He was dimly aware of Mark taking charge of the scene, reporting to law enforcement and requesting an ambulance as sirens sounded in the distance.

Ben shifted as well, blinking to take in Ashley. She was covered in blood and he couldn't tell how much was hers and how much was Sandoval's. Her eyes fluttered open, but her face was pale. "Ashley, oh, God. Where are you hit?"

"Don't rip my clothes off," she said with a weak smile. "It's just my leg. I'll be okay."

He scooped her up into his arms and held her tight to his chest, cradled her like a baby.

"Get the pack out of here," Mark said to Stanley.

"Everybody out," Stanley barked and his pack shifted, slinking out the doors and windows, disappearing before the police arrived. The South American wolves disappeared as well, and Mark let them go. When it came to managing human law enforcement, wolves preferred to handle things on their own.

Mark and Zolla had already put on clothes. His were torn and tangled around his body from when he shifted with them still on. Zolla handed him a pair of pants and took Ashley from his arms while he yanked them on.

"How did you find this place? I didn't give you the address."

"I traced the location on Ashley's phone," he said.

He took Ashley back into his arms. "Thank you," he said, his voice choked.

Mark looked around at the broken windows and bloodstains all over the floor. "This is going to be a hard one to explain."

Ashley's body had begun to shake as shock settled in. Her face grew even paler and she appeared to be losing consciousness.

"Ashley!" he cried.

"Listen to me," Mark said sharply. "Ashley was kidnapped to lure Ben in. He came, but first notified Zolla, who called me. When I arrived, a fight had ensued between the South Americans—some were fighting to help Ben, some against. The windows were broken in the process. I shot Sandoval after he shot Ashley, and the rest of them got away. Got it?"

"Yeah, okay," he said, his heart pinching as he watched Ashley's eyelids slide closed again. The police and ambulance pulled up at the same time and he ran outside, carrying Ashley still crushed against his chest.

"Whoa, whoa, whoa. You never move the victim. Put her down there," one of the EMTs barked, pointing at the grass.

"No," he said in a hard voice, walking straight to the back of the ambulance and stepping in to lay her on the gurney. "You need to help her, right now," he said.

"We'll take care of her," one of them assured her.

"Sir, step away from her please," a cop said, his gun drawn.

Mark appeared at his side, his FBI badge out and on display and took his elbow, leading him away. When Ben shook him off, Mark said in an undertone, "Keep it together, Stone. This is going to be tricky enough as it is."

THE SURGEON WALKED in and gave her a warm smile. "Well, you are one lucky young lady," he said. "Your initial x-rays showed a severe fracture, but when we went in there to put the bone back together, all I found was hairlines. So you don't have any plates or metal in you at all. The bullet is out, and you'll keep this hard cast for six weeks, followed by a soft cast for another four," he said, rapping his knuckles on the cast on her foot.

"What? No color?" she teased. "I wanted pink."

He grinned at her. "I could have a layer of pink added just for you."

She gave him a weak smile. "Thanks."

"The police want to speak with you, and your sister's here. There's also a very anxious man who claims he's your fiancé," he said with a wink.

"When can I get out of here?" she asked, swinging her legs over the side of the bed.

"I can sign your release papers now. I think the

police will want your statement before you can leave though."

"May I see Ben first?"

"I don't see why not," he said, nodding to the medical technician standing behind him. She nodded and left, returning with Ben.

Ben arrived but stopped just in the doorway, looking unsure. She remembered how things had last ended with them and her hand flew to the wounds on her shoulder, which were almost healed. She had forgiven him, but she wasn't about to let it pass without making her feelings clear.

She pushed herself to her feet and marched over to him. "Don't you ever," she said, slapping his chest, "disappear on me—" she struck his shoulder, "again," she said, pushing and shoving at his unmoving form. "You don't get to walk away from me every time things get hard," she said, thumping his chest again and again.

His hands came around her waist, stilling her hips, stroking her gently. "I won't. I won't," he murmured.

His lack of reaction to her tirade made it seem like he wasn't taking her seriously, so she drew back her hand and slapped his face, remembering too late the way wolves re-establish dominance.

She received no alpha reaction this time, though. He just gazed down at her with a pained expression.

"Why did you leave me?" she asked, her eyes suddenly filling with tears.

To her shock, she thought she saw his own eyes grow bright before he blinked rapidly. "I'm sorry I hurt you, Ash. I never wanted that." He shook his head as if disgusted with himself. "I only wanted to protect you, but, as usual, I bungled everything."

She gulped. "You keep pushing me away," she said, her voice cracking.

Ben swung her up into his arms and walked to the bed, where he sat down, keeping her cradled on his lap. "Does that mean you'll have me?" he asked softly.

She resisted a smile as a tear streaked down her cheek. "I'll consider it."

He nibbled at her ear. "I'm not sure you understand how things work here," he said, his voice a deep teasing rumble that made her toes start to curl. "You're mine now. I've laid claim to you. That means you'll never be rid of me, so I suggest you get used to the idea." He pulled away, looking serious. "I hope you can stand me. I know I'm one hell of an asshole, but I promise I'll do everything I can to make you happy. You're all that matters to me. I mean it."

Unaccountably, she burst into tears, all her pent-up emotions flooding out.

Ben appeared alarmed. "I'm so sorry, Ashley. I can't undo marking you, but if the thing that makes you happiest is being rid of me, I'll do my best to stay away," he said, looking sickened by the thought.

She laughed through her tears. "Stupid wolf," she said, wrapping her arms around his neck and burying her face there. "I don't want to be rid of you." She kissed his jaw, then his lips when he turned and captured the back of her head, his concerned look turning to hungry. She pulled away. "I need more of you, not less. Can you give me that?"

He met her eye. "I'll give you everything," he said with the solemnity of a vow.

She laughed and wept more tears, which he thumbed and kissed away.

"Sweet angel. You came into my life like a storm. How did I not know that all I was ever missing was you?"

11

By some miracle, the police seemed satisfied with the story Mark laid out for them. It didn't hurt that Sandoval was a known drug lord, and the DEA was thrilled to have him out of the picture. Ben feared it put him on their watch list as a contact, but since he had nothing to do with drugs or drug running, he hoped it would come to nothing.

He drove Ashley to her home. "Stay there, I will help you out," he said when she started to open the car door.

She ignored him and pushed the door open as he walked around, hopping on one foot as she pulled her crutches from the back seat.

"I said stay," he said, taking them from her hands.

"Woof," she said.

His heart lurched, remembering their first few

days together, the way she had had lit his darkness, her smile quickly becoming something to look forward to, her presence steadying him.

He picked her up, carrying her inside. "It is my job to take care of you, little girl, and I expect your cooperation."

"I have to learn to walk with these things some time," she said.

"Not when I'm around," he said firmly. "And if you need a reminder of how it feels to be over my lap, I won't hesitate to give you one."

Ashley squirmed and her body heated in his arms. The idea of spanking her suddenly appealed, not because he wanted to teach her a lesson, but because he knew it turned her on.

He swung the door shut behind him and carried her to her bedroom where he laid her on her bed.

"So is that how it's going to be with you?" she demanded.

"What?"

"It's your way or I get spanked?"

He smiled, arranging pillows underneath the knee of her wounded leg. "Yeah, pretty much."

"So what happens when I'm mad at you? I think you deserve a spanking for biting me and then just leaving."

He grinned and walked around to stand beside the bed, presenting his ass toward her. "Go ahead."

She gave him a smack. "Ow," she said, shaking her hand out as if it hurt.

He laughed.

"No, really, this isn't fair. What does a she-wolf do to punish her mate?"

He sat down beside her, brushing a strand of her mahogany hair out of her face. "All you have to do is cry," he said softly. "The smell of your tears will bring me to my knees."

She studied him, as if trying to see if he was teasing or not. "So, if I want to end a spanking, all I have to do is cry?" she asked. "Why didn't I try that last time?"

He stroked her cheek. "I don't know if I would end it, but it would be very difficult for me. Bear that in mind when you're naughty, little lady."

"Is that why you seemed so troubled last time?"

He nodded. "I don't want to hurt you," he said seriously. "It kills me to see you cry."

Her lips curved into a sultry smile. "I don't know… I think there were a few times you kinda liked the spanking thing," she said.

He pounced over her, claiming her mouth as one hand worked the buttons on her blouse. "I think that was you," he said between kisses.

"Maybe we should try it out to see," she said, biting down on his lip.

The animal in him jerked with pleasure at the

pain. He growled and yanked open her blouse, popping the rest of the buttons.

"That's two blouses you have destroyed," she complained, although her smile was feral.

"I think the blood had already ruined both before I got to them," he said. His eyes landed on the ugly slashes on the front of her shoulder and he swallowed. He ran a finger over them, surprised the wounds were already closed. They appeared to be two weeks old, not roughly thirty-six hours.

"Didn't Zolla tell you?" she asked. "He thinks I have wolf blood in me and that's why they healed so fast."

A ripple of recognition went through his body. Yes. It made sense she had wolf blood. Why else would he be so drawn to her? He lowered his head and kissed the marks reverentially. "My little wolfling," he murmured. "How can this be?"

"I think it was my grandfather—my dad never knew his father and my grandmother would never say who he was."

"Your dad never shifted?"

"I really don't think so. But he was always very protective of his girls, like you are," she said, touching his face.

He leaned over and kissed her, doing his best to caress her with his lips, instead of attacking. He'd never been one to 'make love'—it wasn't something wolves did, but for her, for his Ashley, he would try.

He slipped her bra down over her shoulders, kissing along her collarbone. Her scent filled his nostrils, intoxicating him. Sliding his body over hers, he ran his thumb lightly over her pebbled nipple, kissing down her throat. She wove her fingers into his hair and arched against his touch. Her skin was impossibly soft, her body so slender and lithe beneath him.

"You're beautiful," he whispered hoarsely.

"You're a fucking God," she answered.

He chuckled. "Language, sweetheart," he warned, flicking his tongue in her ear and nibbling on her lobe. He had her bra off and her skirt up, his index finger stroking along the dampened silk gusset of her panties.

"Fuck, fuck, fuck," she dared, lifting her chin like an insolent child.

He chuckled and sat back, straddling her, and made a show of rolling up his sleeves. "You are determined to have your bottom warmed by me tonight, aren't you?"

Her eyes darkened and she squirmed underneath him. The scent of her arousal reached his nose like nectar.

He pinned her wrists to the bed beside her head. "Where do you think you're going?" he drawled.

She giggled.

He looked into her eyes and lifted his weight off

her just enough to roll her to her belly. "Pull down your panties, Ashley," he murmured, releasing her wrists and climbing off her.

She hesitated.

He waited.

Turning her head to look at him, she lifted her ass in the air and reached down with both hands, sliding her panties down to her thighs.

"Good girl." He grabbed the pillow from the bed. "Lift your hips again," he commanded, and slid the pillow under her pelvis when she complied. He ran his hand over her naked curves, doing his best to ignore the cast on her leg that screamed for him to treat her as fragile. He focused instead on her gorgeous ass, lifted and presented for his chastisement and his cock pushed painfully against his pants.

He brought his palm down, watching her cheek flatten and spring back. He slapped the other side, waiting for the red prints of his fingers to stand out against her milky skin. She wiggled her ass for more. He bit back a groan. Knowing she craved his dominance sent a shot of pure lust rocketing through his body. Wolves were born to dominate, at least alpha wolves were. Having a female who offered herself up the way Ashley did fed some inner source of virile power.

"I think I may have to give you regular spankings," he said, slapping one side of her ass, then the other. "I can't have you acting out just to earn a punishment."

She moaned wantonly.

He picked up the pace, spanking a little harder as he focused on slapping the low middle of her cheeks, just above her sweet little pussy.

"Oh!" she gasped.

"I expect your instant obedience and complete respect, or you'll be spending all your time in the corner with your panties down and a bright red bottom on display."

Ashley made a keening sound, as if she was about to come. He wondered if he could bring her to climax just through spanking. He picked up the intensity a little more, still spanking right over her sex.

Her fingers closed on the sheets, and she lifted her head, giving a throaty cry over and over again. "Rub your clit, Ashley," he commanded, his voice thick.

She didn't seem to understand at first, but he didn't pause the spanking, still paddling her with a steady beat. After a moment, she reached a hand down between her pelvis and the pillows and immediately came undone. Her bottom clenched up, legs straightening as she arched.

He slid his own hand beneath her and shoved her hand aside, vibrating the pad of his finger over her sensitive nub.

She vocalized her release with a louder cry of pleasure, humping his hand as she came. Nothing could be more satisfying than pleasing his female.

"Beautiful girl," he murmured. He caressed her heated cheeks, then slid his fingers between her legs and stroked her swollen, wet pussy.

He'd had her from behind the first time. This time he wanted to see her face. He shucked his clothes and grabbed a condom from his wallet. Rolling her over to her back, he pulled out the pillow and climbed over her.

She took the condom from his hand, ripping open the foil wrapper and rolling the rubber on his cock. He positioned himself directly above her honeyed slit, her heat pulsing against his sensitive organ. She rocked her hips and reached down to guide him in.

He pushed slowly, relishing the moment of entry and the dizzying effect of the walls of her vagina hugging his manhood like a glove. Her fingers tightened on his shoulders and he stopped, giving her a chance to grow accustomed to his size. After a beat, she began to move, lifting her hips to take him deeper.

"That's it, baby," he murmured, ignoring his body's desire to celebrate their union and pound into her without mercy.

She arched, making sweet little moans each time he stroked into her. She lifted her legs in the air and wrapped her ankles behind his back, using them to pull him even deeper, hoisting her pelvis up to meet him.

"Oh, God," he groaned. "I won't make it long at this rate."

Ashley closed her eyes, her hair spread out on the pillow as her head slid up and down with the force of his thrusts. She clutched at his arms, dug her fingernails deep into his flesh, and thrust even harder to meet him. "Give it to me."

"What? Oh, *gawd...*" He slammed into her, losing all ability to regulate his need. Using one hand on her shoulder to pin her in place, he thrust over and over until lights exploded before his eyes and he came, shouting her name.

EVEN IF HER bed were on fire, Ashley couldn't have moved. Every muscle had gone limp in the wake of her orgasm. Her pussy still throbbed from Ben's invasion, stretched wide and punished with his rough lovemaking. Even her insides felt pounded, but she adored the sensation, wished to savor the sensation of being so well-used, so very much his.

He eased out of her and settled at her side, pulling her against him. "Are you okay?"

"Mmm," was all she could manage to say.

"How's your leg? Did I hurt you?"

"Shh," she said, touching his lips. "I'm fine. I'm better than fine; I'm wonderful."

"I love you," he said.

She stopped breathing.

He looked uncertain. "It probably seems way too soon to say something like that, but it's true. Wolves are different. We know our mates from almost the moment we meet them."

She traced the line of his brow. "Does that mean it's fate? Or destiny? I mean, do you think you have only one mate?"

He shrugged. "Yeah, I suppose so. I mean, not all wolves mate for life, but most do. It would have to be pretty bad to call it quits." He frowned, looking lost in thought.

"What?"

He swallowed. "I was just thinking about my mom."

"You think she chose death rather than divorce your dad?"

He nodded. "Divorce would never have been an option with my father. He would've hunted her to the ends of the earth. She was more of a possession than a partner. We all were."

"What happened between your dad and that guy today?"

Ben's face turned stony, as if the memory of her kidnapping angered him.

She stroked his cheek.

"Sandoval led a rival pack to my father's in Caracas. He was a drug lord—filthy rich—and growing more and more powerful every day. My father felt the threat of a takeover and he summoned me back to Caracas to stand beside him in a fight. Leon had moved to the States and made a success for himself, so he wasn't expected back. The idea was always that I would inherit leadership of my father's pack, so it made sense for me to go, but I ignored the summons.

"There were threats—Sandoval issued a challenge, which my father ignored. When I didn't show up, my father took a coward's way out and planned Sandoval's murder. He planted a bomb in his limo, only it exploded with his wife and daughters inside.

"Realizing the shit was going to hit the fan, my father called me back again, desperate this time. I made myself unavailable—I just didn't answer his calls or messages. Leon went instead, and Sandoval killed them both." Ben's mouth twisted into a bitter expression.

"Ben," she said, "their deaths are not your fault or responsibility. You chose not to engage in a fight that wasn't yours and lacked honor. Your brother made a different choice, which was his right. It had nothing to do with you."

"Yes, it did," Ben said, the anger in his face causing her to stiffen. "If I had gone, Leon never would've had to make the choice."

"That's not true. He could've made the same decision as you did. And if you'd gone, he still might have chosen to go. He was his own man—you didn't force him into anything."

Ben's eyes reddened and he fell onto his back, staring at the ceiling.

"Ben, we're each in charge of our own destiny. You're an alpha. A man who follows his own guidance and chooses his own path. You made the right choice. And if you hadn't… then you might not be here today and we never would've met."

Ben rolled back to face her, smothering her with a kiss. "You are my destiny," he said, sounding choked. "After Leon—" He broke off and swallowed. "I couldn't take it that I had lived and he hadn't. He was the better man. He had a wife and children, a successful company, a pack that depended on his leadership. I had nothing—I was nothing. I would've given anything to trade with him—to give my life so that he could've stayed." A tear escaped one of Ben's eyes and rolled down his nose. "But maybe—maybe you're right. Maybe I had a destiny that I just couldn't see at the time." He swiped at the moisture on his cheek. "A future with you."

She swallowed the lump in her throat. "Yes. Your future holds all kinds of successes too."

He smiled and pressed a kiss to her forehead. "You're so precious to me, it hurts."

She blinked up at him, her chest swelling. "So back to this mating for life thing. Are you really my fiancé now, or was that just something you told the doctor to get him to let you into my hospital room?"

Ben grinned. "I'm whatever you want to call me. We don't need human names for relationships. As far as wolves are concerned, I marked you, and you're mine."

She smirked. "Are you calling me a possession?"

He tickled her, causing her to squeal and press her elbows to her ribs in a fruitless attempt to protect herself. "I'm saying you can't get rid of me now. If you need a ring on your finger to believe that, I'll buy you the biggest diamond on earth, but you'd better prepare yourself—I'm not leaving."

"Do you mean prepare my house or my life?" she teased.

"Hmm, that's a good question. Shall I move in here with you, or do you want to move in with me?"

Her heart double-pumped. He meant it—he really wanted them to move in together. "Well… your place is probably a lot nicer," she said.

He smiled. "Actually, it's not. It's just a stupid apartment with the very basics in furniture."

She cocked her head. Why was a multi-million-aire living with the just basics? "Were you punishing yourself?"

He shrugged. "I didn't feel comfortable spending Leon's money."

"Didn't Leon's wife inherit his money?"

"Yes, I mean my salary from Stone."

"That's not Leon's money, that's your salary, for *working*, dummy."

"Uh oh," Ben said, rolling her to her belly and pinning her down with a hand in the middle of her upper back. He delivered a flurry of stinging swats to her still-sore bottom, making her tummy flip like a pancake.

God, she loved his dominance.

"Rule number one, little wolfling. Never call me names." He landed another five spanks, which left her moaning. "You may call me *sir*, or *master*, or *Mr. Stone*."

The word *master* made her pussy clench. She would love to serve Ben Stone as his own personal sex slave.

He climbed over her. "Spread your legs," he murmured in her ear.

She opened her thighs and his cock dived straight back into her pussy, without any guidance.

She sucked in her breath at the sting.

"Are you sore, sweet girl?" he asked.

She hesitated. It hurt, but she wanted him to go on. "No."

He grabbed a fistful of her hair and pulled her head back, growling in her ear, "Was that a lie?"

Her pussy gushed. "Please don't stop," she breathed.

He chuckled. "I might do this all night long if you're not careful."

Her muscles clamped down on his cock in a mini-orgasm. "I won't stop you," she gasped when she could breathe again.

"Let's find a new place to live, together," he said as he glided in and out of her.

Bliss swept over her in waves, long before he slid his hand under her and diddled her clit to set off another earth-shattering orgasm.

12

He pulled up at the warehouse and turned off the engine. He saw both Zolla's and Mark's cars parked in the lot, which was filled with cars and motorcycles. At least he had two friends in there. He had called Stanley and requested a meeting with the pack.

He'd brought Ashley—un-blindfolded this time. She was his mate, so if he was going to be a part of this pack, they'd have to get used to her. Having her along gave him strength. Her very presence made him want to man up where before he had ducked his head.

They walked in and although the sound of conversations didn't diminish, he sensed the attention of most wolves on him. Everyone was there—male and female wolves alike. He caught sight of Shayla across the room and experienced a moment of uncertainty. How would she feel about him taking Leon's place? Lord knew he wasn't half the wolf Leon had been. She gave him a small smile and lifted her fingers in a wave.

He waved back. Zolla came forward, his wiry frame making him look almost adolescent in comparison with the brawny wolves around him, not that human form necessarily correlated with wolf size. He pushed his glasses up on his nose and grinned, sticking out his hand.

Ben grasped his palm. "Thanks for coming. I hope it wasn't awkward," he said, wondering if anyone gave him crap because he'd left their pack.

Zolla shrugged. "I don't care about that," he said. "Hey, Ashley."

Ashley moved in for a hug, and Ben was surprised to find he didn't want to kick the wolf's teeth in. Maybe marking her had eased some of the masculine aggression that had controlled him since the moment he first laid eyes on her. Or perhaps it had been her exquisite surrender the night before.

"How's your leg?"

She grinned. "Doctor said it was miraculous—the bone didn't need the reconstruction the first x-rays showed was necessary."

"You've got good genes, there," Zolla said with a wink.

Ben slid an arm around Ashley's waist and pulled her against his side.

Stanley walked over and shook his hand. "The floor is yours whenever you're ready. Do you want me to introduce you?"

"Nah, that's okay," Ben said, putting two fingers to his lips to whistle. The room fell silent.

"Brothers, sisters," he said. "Thank you all for coming tonight. I came to thank you for standing by me yesterday—sticking your necks out and risking your lives for a guy who hasn't offered this pack one thing. I didn't deserve what you did for me."

No one spoke.

"I haven't participated with the pack as I should have. I know I've failed you and I've failed Leon." His eyes sought Shayla and he found her in the crowd. She gave him a small, encouraging smile. "I want you to know from now on, I'm in, if you'll have me. I'd be honored to be your brother, and serve in whatever way is asked of me."

The room was silent.

"What if you are asked to be alpha?" Stanley asked.

The wolves all stared at him, waiting. He saw challenge in some of their eyes. He met their gazes squarely until one by one, they dropped. He couldn't imagine why they would want him as their leader. He hadn't proven he had any ability to lead. Sure, he was the biggest, strongest wolf, but that didn't mean he had the ability to guide them.

Zolla gave him a nod of encouragement. For

some reason, the omega wolf believed in him. And his friendship had saved both his and Ashley's life the day before.

He bowed his head. "I will serve in whatever way is asked of me, for the good of the pack."

"Leadership requires sacrifice," Stanley said after another long silence. "Yesterday, I saw your willingness to sacrifice yourself to protect your mate. Would you be willing to offer that kind of protection to your pack?"

He looked out over the faces of the pack. They were his kind—his species—wolves living amongst humans. They took care of one another. If they didn't, they risked exposing their secret to the world, which might trigger their extinction. Stanley had been right before—lone wolves were a detriment to all. He had weakened the pack by staying away.

He swallowed. "I would give my life for you, individually and as a whole," he swore solemnly.

He sensed a ripple of approval, although still no one spoke.

"Wolves are not democratic by nature," Stanley said, "but we are Americans, after all. Who here objects to this alpha's rule?"

He scanned the faces. Some of the wolves looked dubious with their arms folded across their chests, but no one dissented.

"I don't have any practice leading a pack," he said, "but I promise to give it my best."

Zolla lowered to one knee and bowed his head, holding his fist in his hand in the position of respect for their alpha. Mark and Stanley went down next. Shayla dropped, too, and strangely, she wore a smile almost like a proud parent might give their new graduate. One by one, the wolves dropped to the floor at his feet, showing their subservience to him.

When even Ashley copied the gesture, balanced on her crutches, a shudder ran through him—a sign of the rightness and importance of the moment.

Humbled, he mimicked the gesture, clasping his fist and bowing his head. "You honor me," he said. "I will do my best to defend and serve you as your leader and your brother wolf." He dropped his head back and howled in the direction of the moon.

The entire pack joined him, raising their voices to mingle with his, filling the metal building with the reverberation of their united song.

When the howls died down, he said, "I will take any old or new business in a moment, but first, I'd like to introduce you to my mate." He reached for Ashley's hand and helped her to her feet. "This is Ashley. She is part wolf and my salvation—the female who rescued me from my worst self. I know humans are not usually a part of these activities, and I know it's unusual for an alpha to mate with a human, but I hope you will make her as welcome as you would a full-blooded wolf." He hardened his gaze as he swept it across the crowd, showing them a hint of warning so they would understand he was giving them an order, not a request.

He squeezed Ashley's hand, sensing her nervousness but knowing she would overcome any objections anyone had about her. Hell, she had won him over in about five seconds flat.

"Does anyone have business that has to be discussed tonight, or can we go straight to the food?" he asked with a grin. Wolf meetings typically included a potluck at the end, in which food was shared, along with socializing. For this meeting, he had told Stanley he'd provide the food, which he'd had catered by a local Mexican restaurant.

"Let's eat," someone called out.

He grinned. "All right, the food's in my car. If a couple of you could give me a hand, I'll get it set up."

Ashley was already swinging her crutches toward the door. He grabbed her waist and pulled her back. "Where do you think you're going?"

"To get the food."

"How exactly were you planning on carrying it?"

She leaned the crutches against the wall. "I don't think I need these things," she said.

He fixed her with a stern look and pointed at the couch. "Sit down and don't move until I come and get you or I will roast your behind."

She looked like she was going to protest, so he

tossed her over his shoulder and carried her to the couch, where he deposited her.

"Stay," he commanded.

She grinned, her blue eyes bright against flushed cheeks. "Woof."

He winked as he headed out to the car where several people already waited to help carry in the food. They made quick work of it, bringing it in and setting it out on folding tables along the back.

Shayla appeared at his side. "It's about time," she said.

"What?"

"This pack has been waiting for you to get your head out of your ass and take charge for three years now," she said, her hands on her hips.

He sucked in his breath. "I don't know how to be like Leon," he said, admitting his biggest concern.

She touched his arm. "You'll be like Ben," she said with a smile. "And that will be enough."

"Thanks," he said, stunned by her vote of confidence.

"Leon would be proud of you," she said. "He always said you'd be great at whatever you decided to do."

Ben blinked and rubbed his nose as his vision went wavy.

Shayla lifted her cheek for the Latin American kiss, then wrapped her arms around him and gave him a hug. "I'm happy for you, Ben." She nodded toward Ashley. "She's obviously wonderful."

"Thanks, Shay. I appreciate it," he said. His chest felt so full and warm he feared it might burst.

He made his way back to Ashley, which took a while, because he had to stop to accept regards from various wolves along the way. When he reached her, he pulled her up to stand and wrapped his arms around her waist, kissing the top of her head.

"Congratulations, alpha," she said.

He cupped the back of her head and tipped it back to kiss her lips. "Thanks for being here with me tonight."

She pressed her torso against his, gazing up into his eyes with a love he didn't deserve. "Thank you for bringing me."

BEN DROVE them to work together the next morning. She felt almost giddy about returning to the office as his mate, rather than just his assistant, although she shuddered to think what everyone would say about her. Obviously there would be the comments about her sleeping her way to the top. And if Ben was set on making changes, she'd be blamed for anything unpopular.

Ben hadn't let her go in the previous day,

insisting that she follow the doctor's orders, despite the fact that the doctor didn't know about her wolf-y healing properties. Now, all her excitement about working for Ben Stone came bubbling back, intensified rather than dimmed by the fact that they were intimate.

Ben had picked out her suit, saying he liked the way her legs looked in it. The beige, fitted ensemble featured a long, slim jacket and short, tight skirt. She'd reminded him that one of her legs was in a cast so the look wouldn't be the same as when she'd worn it the previous week, but he'd just smacked her ass and told her to put it on.

"So, is it back to 'Mr. Stone' when we're in the office?" she asked, watching his profile as he drove.

His lips curled up at the edges. "Yes."

"Ah, and we're also back to the monosyllabic answers?"

His eyes slid sideways and he continued to smirk, but didn't answer.

"And the non-answers." She leaned her head back on the seat and sighed, even as a wave of heat flushed up and down her entire body. How could she really protest when she loved the stern Mr. Stone persona?

"I suppose it's best we keep our relationship a secret while we're at work?" she asked.

Ben looked over, his dark-lashed green eyes

boring into her with their usual intensity. "It's not really anyone's business," he said.

"I know, and it probably won't take long to come out if we're driving in together, but it's probably better to keep it to ourselves, don't you think?"

"Are you asking me or telling me?"

She opened her mouth, then shut it, not sure how to answer.

"Is that what you want?"

She furrowed her brow. What she wanted and what she thought was best were actually two different things. Or rather, she wanted things both ways—she wanted the entire world to know that Ben had chosen her as his mate, but she always wanted to earn the respect of the people she worked with. She sighed. Why were things so complicated for women in the workplace?

"Yeah, I guess so."

Ben shrugged. "All right. I'll try not to rip your little skirts off while we're at the office."

She giggled. "Thanks, I think."

Ben pulled into the lot and they took the elevator up together. She thought about insisting they ride separately, but Ben already looked like he wanted to carry her instead of letting her walk with the crutches, so she kept her mouth shut.

Karen was sitting at her desk when they arrived together, but if she thought it was odd, she didn't show it.

Ben carried her bag into the office and set it down. "Need anything?"

"What? *You're* going to get *me* coffee?"

"If you ask nicely." He lowered his voice. "Maybe if you pull up your skirt just a little bit?"

Her face grew warm and she picked up a pen and tossed it at him. "Get out. I do the coffee running around here. Do you need some?"

He grinned. "No." He leaned in her doorway, contemplating her for a moment.

Her body temperature rose by several degrees, warmed by his hungry look. Her mouth opened, but all thoughts and words had flown away.

Ben winked, lifting his large frame from the doorway with a grace that belied his size. He walked away, taking her breath with him.

She sat down at her desk, smiling. She loved her life.

About forty minutes later, Ben called. "Come into my office."

She picked up her laptop but quickly realized she couldn't carry it and use her crutches. Abandoning the laptop, she hobbled over to his office.

"Shut the door, Ashley," he said.

She swung it shut.

"You're too far away over there," he said, lifting his chin in the direction of her office.

She did her best to saunter with the crutches and dropped into his lap. "Is this close enough?"

she asked, pitching her voice to a low and seductive note.

"Not quite."

She leaned over and kissed his neck. "How about this?"

"Mmm, I'm not sure."

She sank to her knees at his feet and bit his trousers at the crotch, hoping her hot, moist breath reached his cock through the fabric. "How about this?"

His manhood strained against his pants. He groaned. "That might be too close," he said in a strangled voice. Grasping her forearms, he lifted her back onto his lap.

She faked a pout.

"Don't worry, my little assistant. I will be demanding all kinds of service like that from you." He ran his thumb over her lower lip. "In fact, just this morning I resolved to have you in every single room of this building. That means every floor, every cubicle, every bathroom, every conference room, maybe even the closets, too. How long do you think that will take us?"

Her pussy pulsed, already readying for his suggested activity.

"I-I'm not sure," she managed to say.

"Well, I'd like you to calculate it, Ashley. I need a checklist to work from. On my desk by close of business, understand?"

Her pelvic floor lifted as the walls of her vagina fluttered. "Yes, sir," she breathed.

"But right now, I had the other sort of work on my mind."

She straightened up. "What can I do for you, Mr. Stone?" she asked, still using her sultry tone.

"Did you ever put together that report on who I need to cut from middle management?"

"Yes, sir, would you like me to go get it?"

"Please," he said, keeping his hands on her hips as she stood. "And then come back right *here*," he said, pulling her back to sit on his lap momentarily.

She giggled.

"Oh, I have all kinds of plans for you right here in this office," he said wickedly. "I seem to recall you were asking whether you'd be spanked on the job?"

Her grin stretched even wider, lust flaming hotter.

He waggled his eyebrows. "You'd better dot your i's and cross your t's, Ms. Bell, or I'll have you bent over this desk with your panties down before you can say 'yes, sir,' and you know Karen would hear everything."

Her face grew warm, pulse racing. "I'll be right back with that report, Mr. Stone," she said, abandoning the crutches in favor of covering her ass and shooting him a look of pure heat over her shoulder.

～

BEN SHIFTED in his seat to accommodate his hardened cock. Working with Ashley was going to make every day torturous pleasure. It seemed strange how different he felt about working at Stone that day. He was a completely different person now. He was finally not just ready, but enthusiastic to do right by his brother's company.

Ashley returned, carrying her laptop and he realized she wasn't using her crutches. He shouldn't have sent her running back and forth—he should have just gone into her office, but he knew she loved the boss/assistant dynamic.

She dropped back into his lap.

He breathed in the scent of her hair and wrapped his arms around her.

She opened her laptop and he looked over her shoulder as she pulled up her report. "This is the list. I put them in order of salaries, highest to lowest, then it lists their name, title, and the reason I think they aren't performing or should be cut."

He scrolled through the list, skimming. It appeared she based the decisions on missed performance targets, lagging sales, over-budget spending, and turnover within their department.

"How long did it take you to put this together?"

"Well, I worked on it all last week, so about thirty hours to gather and analyze all the necessary data."

"Okay. Send the report to Beth in human resources and ask her to make the cuts."

Ashley tensed. "Wait—you're just going to make the cuts? Based solely on my opinion?"

"Yes. Why shouldn't I?"

"Well, we're talking about people's livelihoods here. I'm not sure I'm really qualified to make these final decisions. I was just making a recommendation for you to review and make up your own mind."

"And I trust your recommendation. Do you need to revise it now that you know that you're making the final call?"

She looked at him with her eyes wide, then began to scroll through her report with a frantic air. After a moment, she looked back up. "No."

He smiled. "So you gave me your best recommendation the first time?"

"Yes, sir."

"Good girl."

She flushed, looking pleased.

"Now, Ashley, we need to discuss something."

"Yes, sir?"

"One of your most important jobs, as my assistant and as my fiancée, is to protect me from my own mistakes. So if I do something dumb like ask you to bring me a report when I ought to know that you can't possibly bring your laptop and use your crutches, it's your job to let me know that so I don't feel like an ass when I figure it out for myself."

She smiled and dropped her eyes. "I'm feeling very unsexy with these stupid things," she said.

He lifted her off his lap and turned her to fold over his desk. Pulling up her skirt, he slowly slid her silky pink panties down to her thighs. "Let me just show you what will happen if I catch you walking without them again," he said, standing and opening his desk drawer, where he found an eighteen-inch wooden ruler, two inches wide and one-eighth inch thick.

He brought it down smartly across her exposed buttocks.

She gasped, squeezing her cheeks together. "Ben," she whispered. "Karen will hear."

"Hmm," he said, pulling her panties back up and trying again. The sound was slightly more muffled.

She gasped again, lurching forward.

He tapped the ruler on her bottom. "I may have to find something to make an impression that's quieter to keep here in my office for when you misbehave."

Ashley moaned and the scent of her arousal filled his nostrils.

"Because I want to be able to provide you with instant feedback on your performance here in the office," he said, smacking her once more, much harder this time.

Ashley squeaked.

He peeled her panties back down, dragging them off over her bulky cast. "Spread your legs, Ash," he murmured.

Her intake of breath excited him. He dug a condom out of his pocket and unzipped his pants, sheathing his eager cock. He rubbed the head of his penis over her pussy, teasing her clit and spreading her moisture up and down. "I'm going to use a condom today, but there may be times I choose to fill you with my seed," he warned.

He made a note to have a genuine discussion about birth control with her later, but at this moment, threatening her with the danger of bearing his pups turned him on, and based on her pussy's release of fresh lubricant, had the same effect on her.

He pressed against her entrance, parting her inner lips. She stretched to allow his entrance, her heat engulfing his cock. He pushed all the way in and gripped her hair, tugging her head back. "Who do you belong to?" he demanded, easing out and burying himself once more in her sweet passage, even deeper this time.

"You," she gasped.

He pumped a little faster, not releasing her hair. "Say *I belong to Ben Stone*."

Her pussy gushed moisture. "I belong to Ben Stone."

He lost his breath. Letting go of her hair, he

wrapped his arm around her hips to keep from slamming her pelvis against the hard wood of his desk as he took her roughly, plowing in and out, burying his cock in her heat over and over again until the sound of her throaty cry made him lose all control. He shot his load, all the while continuing to stroke in and out. He reached around between Ashley's legs and pinched her clit. She clamped her lips around a scream, bucking under him, the walls of her sex contracting around his member, wringing every last drop of his cum from his cock.

A few minutes later when they'd cleaned up, he pulled her back to his lap in the chair. "Do you suppose Karen heard that?" he teased.

"Oh, God, what are you doing to me?"

"Just making sure you understand your extensive duties around here."

She turned around, kneeling on either side of his seat and pressing her breasts into his face. "I am at your disposal, Mr. Stone," she said.

He squeezed and kneaded her ass, already ready for another round. "Damn," he groaned. "You're about to get yourself fucked again."

"Should I leave?"

He groaned again—her smell making him dizzy, the feel of her soft curves under his hands too much to give up. With effort he released her. "You'd better put your panties back on and then sit on the desk out of my reach."

"Yes, sir," she murmured. She complied, arranging herself on his desk with her sleek legs crossed, the cast dangling on the bottom. "Did you have something else to discuss?"

He gathered his thoughts and cleared his throat. "Yes. I was thinking after work we could go look for houses. Or would you like to have one built?"

Her face lit up. "Ooh, really? For us to live in?"

He grinned. "Yeah."

"Building a house would be fun," she said with her eyes shining.

"What are you thinking?"

"Something up in the foothills with a wall of windows and a great view."

"And a swimming pool?"

"How'd you know I swim?"

He grinned. "You told me you took State in high school. Besides, you're my mate. It's my job to know things about you."

She slid off the desk and dropped back into his lap, pressing her lips to his mouth. "You never stop surprising me."

"Good," he said. "I intend to keep you on your toes. If we're not house-hunting, maybe we can find that ring for your finger this evening instead."

Ashley flushed. "I don't really need a ring. I didn't mean to make it seem like—"

He cut her off with a kiss. "No, you're getting a ring. And a proper wedding as is human custom.

Unless—" He hesitated, suddenly unsure. "Unless I'm going too fast and you want some more time to think about it."

Ashley snorted. "I thought it was a done deal," she said, touching the marks on her shoulder.

"For me it is, but I understand if you need more time."

She gazed into his green eyes, losing herself in their warmth. "Thank you, but the way I understood it, I already belong to Ben Stone, so I don't see any sense in resisting." She smiled. "But maybe a long engagement would give my family and friends time to get to know you and adjust to the idea."

He tucked a curl behind her ear. "Sounds perfect to me, sweetheart."

"Shouldn't you propose or something?"

"Oh," he said, straightening. "Sorry." He cleared his throat. "Ashley Bell, I need you in my life. I need you by my side at work and in my bed at night. I need to be near you, to breathe your scent and touch your skin for the rest of my days on this earth. If you will take me as your husband and mate, I promise I will work every day to keep a smile on your lips, to fill your home with my love, and to give you my very best. I will provide for you and protect you, I will learn to give you what you need and what you desire, and I will never, ever stray. Will you please have me?"

"Jesus."

"What?"

"That was the best proposal I've ever heard in my life. I wish I'd recorded it."

"Are you going to answer me?"

She cupped his face. "My answer is yes, wolf. I will be your wife and your mate. I will do my best to serve you, to fill your home with love and little baby wolves."

"Pups," he corrected her, blinking rapidly.

"Do you want pups?" she asked softly.

This time she saw actual tears pop into his eyes before he blinked them back. "I never did… but now—" He stopped and swallowed. "Yeah. I would love that."

"Then yes. My answer is yes. I'm yours, Ben Stone. In every way possible."

"Ashley," he murmured, reaching for her face. He met her lips with his, kissing her softly at first, then with more force. "My forever Ashley. I love you, sweetheart."

"And I love you," she said, trying to impart the full promise of her words in the strength of her gaze as she moved in for one more kiss.

THANK you for reading *Alpha's Hunger*! Read the

sexy-spanky bonus book featuring Ben and Ashley in Alpha's Punishment.

WANT MORE? ALPHA'S PUNISHMENT

It started with a small deception…

Now, five long months later, Ashley's alpha shifter fiancé still thinks they've been trying to conceive a pup when she's secretly been taking the pill the whole time. When he finds out, there's going to be hell to pay, and that means a hot punishment from her dominant wolf.

The characters from Renee Rose's steamy romance The Alpha's Hunger return in a short story full of sex, spankings, and hard, dominant lovemaking.

NOTE: This book was originally published by Stormy Night Publications in 2015 and the text has not been altered since the first edition. The Alpha's Punishment includes spankings and rough, intense sexual scenes. If such material offends you, please don't buy this book.

READ NOW —> https://geni.us/apunishment

WANT FREE RENEE ROSE BOOKS?

Go to http://subscribepage.-com/alphastemp to sign up for Renee Rose's newsletter and receive a free copy of *Alpha's Tempta-*

tion, Theirs to Protect, Owned by the Marine, Theirs to Punish, The Alpha's Punishment, Disobedience at the Dressmaker's and *Her Billionaire Boss*. In addition to the free stories, you will also get special pricing, exclusive previews and news of new releases.

Shifter Ops

Alpha's Moon

Alpha's Vow

Alpha's Revenge

Alpha's Fire

Alpha's Rescue

Alpha's Command

Werewolves of Wall Street

Big Bad Boss: Midnight

Big Bad Boss: Moon Mad

Alpha Doms Series

The Alpha's Hunger

The Alpha's Promise

The Alpha's Punishment

The Alpha's Protection (Dirty Daddies)

Two Marks Series

Untamed

Tempted

Desired

Enticed

Wolf Ranch Series

Rough

Wild

Feral

Savage

Fierce

Ruthless

Contemporary

Chicago Sin

Den of Sins

Rooted in Sin

Made Men Series

Don't Tease Me

Don't Tempt Me

Don't Make Me

Chicago Bratva

"Prelude" in Black Light: Roulette War

The Director

The Fixer

"Owned" in Black Light: Roulette Rematch

The Enforcer

The Soldier

The Hacker

The Bookie

The Cleaner

The Player

The Gatekeeper

Alpha Mountain

Hero

Rebel

Warrior

Vegas Underground Mafia Romance

King of Diamonds

Mafia Daddy

Jack of Spades

Ace of Hearts

Joker's Wild

His Queen of Clubs

Dead Man's Hand

Wild Card

Daddy Rules Series

Fire Daddy

Hollywood Daddy

Stepbrother Daddy

Master Me Series

Her Royal Master

Her Russian Master

Her Marine Master

Yes, Doctor

Double Doms Series

Theirs to Punish

Theirs to Protect

Holiday Feel-Good

Scoring with Santa

Saved

Other Contemporary

Black Light: Valentine Roulette

Black Light: Roulette Redux

Black Light: Celebrity Roulette

Black Light: Roulette War

Black Light: Roulette Rematch

Punishing Portia (written as Darling Adams)

The Professor's Girl

Safe in his Arms

Sci-Fi

Zandian Masters Series

His Human Slave

His Human Prisoner

Training His Human

His Human Rebel

His Human Vessel

His Mate and Master

Zandian Pet

Their Zandian Mate

His Human Possession

Zandian Brides

Night of the Zandians

Bought by the Zandians

Mastered by the Zandians

Zandian Lights

Kept by the Zandian

Claimed by the Zandian

Stolen by the Zandian

Rescued by the Zandian

Other Sci-Fi

The Hand of Vengeance

Her Alien Masters

USA TODAY BESTSELLING AUTHOR RENEE ROSE loves a dominant, dirty-talking alpha hero! She's sold over two million copies of steamy romance with varying levels of kink. Her books have been featured in USA Today's *Happily Ever After* and *Popsugar*. Named Eroticon USA's Next Top Erotic Author in 2013, she has also won *Spunky and Sassy's* Favorite Sci-Fi and Anthology author, *The Romance Reviews* Best Historical Romance, and has hit the *USA Today* list fifteen times with her Bad Boy Alphas, Chicago Bratva, and Wolf Ranch series.

Renee loves to connect with readers!
www.reneeroseromance.com
reneeroseauthor@gmail.com

facebook.com/reneeroseromance
instagram.com/reneeroseromance
bookbub.com/authors/renee-rose